TOUGH

CRIME STORIES

TOUGH

A journal of crime fiction and occasional reviews.
www.toughcrime.com

Publisher/Editor: Rusty Barnes
Design: Sue Miller
Contributing Editor: Tim Hennessy

ISBN-13:978-0692166543 (Redneck Press)
ISBN-10:0692166548

Published by Tough in cooperation with Redneck
Press; copyright 2018 Redneck Press and respec-
tive authors

The following are works of fiction. Characters,
events, and organizations are products of the
author's imagination or are used fictitiously.

ADDRESS:
  Tough c/o Rusty Barnes
  119 Bradstreet Avenue
  Revere MA 02151

Contents

◇◇◇◇◇◇

Texas Hot Flash

Michael Bracken

◇◇◇◇◇◇

Sunshine McCall—Sunshine Petunia McCall—stared hard at 40, at the crow's feet collecting in the corners of her weary blue eyes, at the strawberry blonde hair that was now more Clairol than natural, and at the dewlap that had begun to soften the once-firm line of her jaw. Forty looked exactly like 39, but felt a decade older.

She grabbed two tampons from the box under the sink and stuffed them in her pocket. Then she strapped on her holster, checked her weapon, and headed outside to her year-old Maxima.

The drive across town barely outlasted a Tuesday two-fer from Tommy James and the Shondells on her favorite oldies station, and McCall pulled into the employee parking lot just as the local weather report began. She listened to predictions of triple digit heat by mid-afternoon before climbing out of her car and walking inside.

She found a sign taped to her locker, a bad photocopy of her photograph from thirteen years earlier when she'd joined the force fresh from the police academy. Someone with a shaky hand had written "Lordy, Lordy, look who's 40!" above the photograph. The sign looked like the work of the civilian receptionist, a blue-haired woman who had worked at the station since Heck was a pup. McCall tore the paper down, wadded it into a ball, and threw it toward the trashcan.

She missed.

After she clocked in and picked up the keys to her cruiser, McCall spent a moment chewing the fat with the patrol sergeant, a crew-cut Vietnam vet who had killed more men in the line of duty than he had killed during his brief tour in country.

"Any special plans for tonight?" he asked.

"I'm going to slap a T-bone on the grill, microwave a potato, and wash everything down with a six-pack of Lone Star," McCall said.

"Beats the hell out of my fortieth," the patrol sergeant said. "My old lady took me out for Mexican food. Over sopapillas, she said she was leaving me for my son's third grade teacher. I haven't looked at Mex food the same since."

"Women," McCall said. "Go figure."

The patrol sergeant's laugh let her know that he appreciated the sentiment, so she joined him.

Later, alone in her patrol car tagging motorists with her radar gun as they crested the hill near Wal-Mart, McCall glanced at her reflection in the rearview mirror and pondered her need to denigrate other women when surrounded by police officers. She cut her thoughts short when a minivan crested the hill at seventeen miles over the posted speed limit. McCall pulled onto the road behind it and flipped on her lights.

Half a block later, in front of Lowe's on the other side of the Franklin Avenue intersection, the driver pulled her vehicle to the shoulder. After McCall keyed the license plate into her computer and discovered the plate number was clean, she stepped out of her cruiser. As she approached the minivan, the driver's door opened and a pudgy brunette swung her leg out.

"Stay in the car, ma'am!" McCall instructed.

The driver hesitated, and then drew her leg back inside and pulled the door closed. She was rolling her window down when McCall reached the door.

"I'm sorry," the driver said. "I didn't realize—"

McCall cut her off. "License," she said. "Proof of insurance."

"Sure. Yes. I have those," the woman said as she dug through a suitcase-sized purse. McCall watched the woman closely, her hand on the butt of her side-arm, prepared to draw if anything unexpected came out of the purse.

In the back seat, a baby of indeterminate gender began to fuss, sounding as if it was working itself up for a serious wail. The driver stopped fishing through her purse and handed a wad of things through the open window.

McCall took the woman's driver's license and proof of insurance, carried them to the cruiser, and keyed the information into her computer. The driver had no wants or warrants, so McCall wrote a ticket and carried it back to the driver. By then the back-seat baby was at full volume and the woman was anxiously shaking a stuffed rabbit in its face.

"Sign here," McCall said over the baby's screams.

The woman turned, hastily scribbled her name at the bottom of the ticket, and took her copy from McCall's hand a moment later.

McCall returned to her cruiser, drove to a small diner where she knew the restrooms were kept clean, and called in to say she would be out of pocket for a few minutes. Inside the restroom, a one-seater with a secure door, McCall stripped off her holster and used the facilities. Then she changed her tampon. Her flow had started the day before, six days later than usual, and she would have worried about pregnancy if there had been a man in her life.

Instead, she attributed her increasingly erratic cycle to the same source as the midnight sweats and the mid-afternoon hot flashes.

As she pulled from the diner's parking lot, McCall spotted a faculty parking sticker on the rear window of the Lexus in front of her and wondered what subject the driver taught at the local university.

Her brother Moonbeam Able McCall—M. Able McCall on his academic papers, Dr. McCall to his students, and Abe to his friends—taught medieval literature at a liberal arts college in Wisconsin. They hadn't spoken since their parents' funeral following their death in an automobile accident. Their parents had been returning from a WTO protest in Seattle when an intoxicated high school student T-boned their Volkswagen Vanagon at a poorly lit intersection.

After the funeral, after everyone had returned home and she was left with her brother in the only building that remained at the commune where they had been raised, he called her a "sell-out."

They had stood toe-to-toe while he accused her of perpetuating the growing police state, of violating the civil liberties of the innocent and underprivileged, and of betraying their parents' ideals. After the first two minutes, McCall imagined seven different ways she could put her brother facedown on the floor without breaking a sweat. Then she smiled and walked to her room, packed her suitcase, and carried it to the rental car. Moonbeam followed her like a yapping Chihuahua until she opened the car door and turned to face him.

"Bite my ass," she told her brother before climbing into the car and driving away.

The first time she'd left the commune—a patch of land on the northern California coast halfway between Mendocino and Ft. Bragg—McCall had been squeezed in the backseat of Ford Pinto, unaware of its flammability. A long, circuitous route took her from the commune, through the coffee shops of San Francisco, to performing as the lead singer in a Jefferson Airplane/Grateful Dead cover band that toured the U.S. for a year before collapsing under its own pretentiousness following a Saturday evening gig at a Holiday Inn just north of San Antonio.

She bounced from job to job until a one-night-stand's off-hand comment about her conservative opinions led her to the police academy.

Since then, she'd spent more than her share of time in redneck bars where overly familiar men called her "Sunny" and invited her to ride their moustaches. Sunny? She'd never been Sunny, not even as a round-faced hippie child attending the small-town school where the commune sent its children in their peasant dresses and hemp sandals.

That life had been long ago and far away, a time when her parents' generation believed they could change the world by wearing blue jeans and love beads. Except for a few holdouts, those same people were now worried about Social Security and Medicare Part B. Instead of protesting against the pigs, they were demanding better police protection from departments straining under the weight of increased need and decreased budgets.

Sweat rolled from McCall's armpits and stained the elastic of her bra. Her hair clung to her forehead and she pushed it away before reaching for the controls on the cruiser's air conditioning. She pushed the fan to its highest setting. The air conditioning in the car hadn't been designed to combat central Texas's triple digit summer heat, and the fan did little more than shift tepid air from one part of the cruiser to another.

An hour after leaving the diner, McCall responded to a domestic dispute and was the first officer on the scene. She pulled her cruiser to the curb and stepped out. As she pushed the door closed, a large man burst from the house. He had shoulder-length hair, glassy eyes, and a fat roll that obscured his belt. He stood on the porch waving an automatic nearly engulfed by his meaty fist.

McCall pulled her sidearm and dropped behind her cruiser. She rested her forearms on the fender as she drew down on the man. The metal seared her bare forearm but she didn't flinch.

"Put the gun down!" she commanded. "Put the God-damned gun down!"

The man stared at her as if he didn't understand what she was telling him.

A woman with a baby on her hip stepped onto the porch behind him. McCall no longer had a clean shot.

"Put the gun down, Harry," the woman implored. Her voice sounded like fingernails on a chalkboard.

A second police cruiser slid to a halt behind McCall's and the patrol sergeant slipped from it.

"Put the gun down!" McCall shouted again.

Harry raised his hand and the sergeant shot him in the forearm. When he dropped the gun and collapsed on the porch, his wife ran to him.

"Nice shot," McCall told the sergeant.

He glared at her. "I missed. I was aiming at his chest."

McCall radioed for an ambulance as the sergeant approached the wounded man, kicked away the automatic, and suffered the verbal abuse of the man's wife.

After the ambulance had taken the fat man away and the scene had been secured, McCall returned to the station to prepare an incident report.

The bluehaired civilian receptionist gave her a chocolate cupcake with a single burning candle and sang "Happy Birthday" in a warbly voice.

McCall thanked her, blew out the candle without making a wish, ate the cupcake, and sat at her desk until she completed the paperwork required following any officer-involved shooting. She never mentioned the sergeant's comment that he'd missed.

After she completed the paperwork, she stepped into the institutional gray women's restroom, changed her tampon, and returned to the streets.

Nothing much happened the next few hours and McCall returned home after the end of her shift, slapped an inch-thick steak on the grill, and sat on the back porch killing her first Lone Star while the steak sizzled. She could hear children playing in the next yard, heavy metal music from down the street, and dogs barking somewhere in the distance. What she couldn't hear were her own thoughts.

Forty was better that way.

◇◇◇◇◇◇

Night Drive

JM Taylor

◇◇◇◇◇◇

It was the first time Charlie had driven alone at night, and of course he got lost. In high school, he'd never needed to drive—he had a bus or his mom or dad had driven him to practice. Now, he had to get to the college pool on his own. It was the same one he'd swum in for years, following the same coach from one level to another. But he'd never paid attention to when they turned onto which streets. In the dark, he missed first one turn, then tried to make up for it by making another one at random. Within minutes, he was in a canyon of looming triple-deckers. Cars clogged both sides of the street, and every time he slowed to see about making another turn, the line of drivers behind him honked their horns and flashed their lights.

Charlie's eyes darted frantically from the windshield to the rear-view to the side mirror. His hands were frozen at 10 and 2, and he couldn't even pull over to look at his phone. He had no choice but to barrel on blindly, dodging double-parked cars and glaring pedestrians. He prayed for a traffic light, or a parking lot, anywhere he could stop, but it was like he'd been dumped into a bobsled track, and he couldn't stop until he reached the end.

Finally, he came to an intersection he vaguely remembered. A voice—his mother's, his conscience, Jiminy Cricket—told him that turning left was the right answer, so he flicked on the blinker and banged around the corner. He hoped none of the cars behind him was a police officer, ready to nab him for signaling at least 100 feet before his maneuver.

He found himself on a wide road, brightly lit, but no less crowded. He wove with the traffic, realizing this wasn't the road he thought it was. So much for the smart college freshman. The buildings grew seedier and seedier. The blue lights of a cop car appeared in his rear-view, and he had just enough time to clear out of the lane before it flew by him. A pair of creepy looking thugs stared at him from the dark recessed doorway of an apartment building. He locked the doors. He waited like an idiot while three cars took advantage of his getting sidelined before he got back on the road.

His phone buzzed in his pocket. That would be his mom, whose book club was meeting tonight. The clock on the dash said it was 9:30, and he was over an hour late getting home.

Finally, he approached an intersection he knew, where one corner of the zoo intruded into the wasteland. Back in familiar territory, he was fifteen minutes from home. He still had to contend with the crazy drivers—didn't anyone in this neighborhood take driving lessons?—and with the panhandler stalking the lines of stopped cars, but at last he was safe.

He idled ten cars back from the light, his blinker flashing dutifully. The panhandler made his way from car to car, shaking a large Dunkin' Donuts cup. Once he leaned into a window and took a bill. No, Charlie realized, it wasn't a guy, but a girl covered with a long ratty coat too heavy for this time of year. It flashed through his mind that begging at cars was safe enough for winos and homeless men, but a girl could get into so much more trouble.

Her hair fell from under a filthy Yankees cap that covered most of her face, except for the hardened frown and an incongruously delicate chin. His horror grew when she got closer to his car and his headlights illuminated her face. Along with the pretty chin, a splash of freckles across the bridge of her nose gave her something of a cute raccoon's face. Despite the rags and dirt, she was beautiful.

And familiar. It took him a second, but then he realized that she'd once been in his English class. Last year, or eleventh grade? She'd been there only a short time, and the teacher hadn't even commented when she'd disappeared, as if she'd never been there. But her seat had been left vacant, and his eyes had often traveled to it, like a tongue poking into the socket of a lost tooth.

The sad-eyed girl got to his window. Charlie wondered what to do. Give her something? Shake his head the way his father did, and pretend otherwise not to see her? That voice was giving him nothing. Before he could decide, she'd spotted him. Worse, she remembered his name.

"Charlie!" she called. The light changed, and he had a brief window to take off. But then she was standing in front of him, and he was immobilized. Drivers behind him started honking, and he panicked. His foot slipped off the brake, and he almost hit her. "Wait!" the girl screamed, and she dashed to the passenger door, trying to climb in. Charlie bit his lip, realized he couldn't ignore her, and unlocked the door. In a second, she was in, and he was pulling away before she shut the door. He saw too late that he'd run a red light.

"Wow, am I glad you happened by. It isn't really your neighborhood, is it?"

"It's your lucky night," he giggled nervously. He wondered how he could ask her what her name was without offending. "What were you doing there anyhow?"

"Just getting some spare change," she said. "I'm saving up." He couldn't tell if she was serious or not. After a second she said, "I can tell you don't remember me. No worries. I'm Leah."

"Right! Did you switch schools?"

"Something like that."

They were almost at Charlie's house, the journey through the ghetto fading like a bad dream. "What were you really doing in that neighborhood?" he asked. "My dad says when he was a kid, you couldn't walk a block without getting jumped. Gangs and shit."

"Visiting a friend. Listen, Charlie, can you do me a favor? I have something I need to take care of. Could you give me a ride home?"

"Well, it's late. I need to get the car to my mom."

"It's on the way. We're almost there. Please?"

"Yeah, sure. Of course."

She smiled and settled back in her seat. "I knew I could depend on you, Charlie."

She guided him through a section of town he'd never been in. Unlike his own spacious neighborhood, here the houses were tiny cardboard boxes shoved up against each other, or long blocks of old apartment buildings. She led him deeper into the warren of crowded blocks until she said, "Stop here."

"That's your house?" he looked at a grim little cottage with a rusted chain link fence and a car older than either of them in the driveway.

"No, I'm over there." She pointed down the block to a house that might have been the first one's twin. "Just don't want anyone to know I'm here. Wait for me."

"I really need to go. . ."

"Two minutes. I'll be right back."

She got out, and Charlie watched her skulk through the shadows. She scanned the block to make sure no one was watching. Satisfied, she edged up the driveway to a darkened window. She stood on a water spigot for a boost, slid the window up, and swung her leg into the opening. She did it so smoothly, Charlie imagined she must have had a lot of practice.

But then it occurred to him, this might not be her house at all. Was she a burglar, hiring him as her getaway driver? He flushed, and it seemed as though all his pores opened at once, soaking through his shirt. Would anybody be able to identify his car? He turned on the radio to drown out the noise in his head.

Five minutes later, she was sliding into the seat next to him. "Thanks," she said, giving him a kiss on the cheek.

"That really your house?" he said, starting the car.

"You think I'd break into someone else's?"

"Uh, yeah?"

"I didn't even really break in, anyhow. My little sister leaves the window in her room unlocked. This time of night, my father's plastered in the living room, but he keeps a Glock on the table right next to his glass. If I went in the front door, I'd be dead."

"Seriously?" But when she didn't answer, he said more calmly. "So why'd you make me wait?"

She looked down guiltily. Charlie thought she was lovely, despite the grime. "I need you to take me one more place."

"Leah, I can't."

"OK, then just let me ride with you a little way. For company."

He pulled away from the curb and started home. It was already after ten. They passed through a wooded area, where the road slalomed and Charlie could imagine he was driving in Le Mans. If only he could go faster. "I'm going to have to let you out soon. How are you going to get home from here?" he asked.

"Oh, my God! Pull over!" Leah shouted. In a panic, Charlie heaved to the side of the road, forgetting entirely to signal. The front wheel dipped into a drainage ditch.

Panting, he looked at her. "What? What is it?"

"It's really important," she said, leaning close. Her breath tickled his ear. "Do you have a rubber?"

"What?"

"Never mind," she smirked. She pulled a glove from an inside pocket of her coat and snapped it on. Still breathing in his ear, she reached down and popped the button on his jeans and wriggled her fingers into his Y-front. "I always liked you," she cooed. Terrified and excited, he was instantly hard, but it took only a few seconds for him to come. He flushed with shame, but her giggle was encouraging, and she lightly kissed his cheek. "You taste like chlorine," she whispered. "Fresh and clean."

She rolled the glove off, catching most of the come, and tied it up. He stuffed himself back inside, horrified to think what would happen when his mother climbed into the car tomorrow. Would she see the stain he'd surely left?

"Now about that other stop" Leah said, dropping the glove out the window.

"Uh, sure. Of course." His throat was dry and he was afraid he'd hyperventilate. He hit the gas a little too hard, and they bounced out of the gully. Finally, he eased off and was able to keep a steady speed.

Before she could tell him where they were headed, his phone was ringing again. "You gonna answer that?" Leah asked.

Charlie gripped the wheel with one hand and put the other in his pocket. Just the thought that her hand had been there only a minute ago made him stiffen again. He slid the phone out and answered it. "Hi, mom."

"Charlie! Where the hell are you? I've been trying to call you for an hour. Are you OK? What happened? Why aren't you home yet?"

In the seat next to him, Leah giggled again, and he glared at her to shut up.

"I, uh, got a little lost. I had to give a ride to one of my friends, and he didn't know how to direct me. I should be home in..." He looked at Leah for a number.

"An hour," she mouthed, finishing it with a silent kiss.

"Uh, just a few minutes. I think I know where I am right now."

"Do you see any landmarks?"

"Ma, I have to go. I shouldn't talk and drive. I'll be home soon." He dropped the phone, and Leah helpfully hung it up for him.

"Didn't realize I was corrupting you," she said.

"Listen, it's really late, and she's never going to let me use the car again. Where are we going? Where's this errand?"

"Turn here," she said. Her voice sounded choked, so he complied, and they left the woods for one of the main roads. They drove past darkened stores and empty lots. After a few blocks, he said, "What did you get at your house, anyway?"

"Nothing much. Some of my mother's jewelry."

"So you were stealing?"

"Just keep driving." She gave him directions to an address in the next town. When they got there, Charlie wasn't too surprised to find an abandoned strip mall. One window had a sign that promised "Coming Soon!", but it had faded and half fallen. Charlie pulled into a space, still careful to stay inside the lines.

"OK, wait here," Leah said.

"Now what? Where are you going?"

"Around back. Don't worry, I'll be fine." She opened her coat, and he saw the hilt of a hunting knife in her belt.

"What the fuck!" he cried.

"I said don't worry. Just don't leave without me. Be right back." And again, she was gone, disappearing behind a dumpster.

He spent an anxious five minutes ignoring the ringing of his phone. How long ago had he told his mother "a few minutes"? It was nearly midnight. Then he heard shouting, and a short scream. He hesitated, then jumped out of the car.

Two snarling voices echoed in the dark. He rushed towards the shadows behind the dumpster, just as he heard the thump of a fist hitting bone. He rounded the corner, and saw Leah dazed, slumping against the wall. The orange glow of a useless security light illuminated a nasty cut oozing on her cheek. Her eyes flew open and flicked to one side, trying to get him to leave, but it was too late.

Across from her, a guy in a worn leather coat bent half over, guttural moans of pain, or anger, cascading from his maw. Leah must have kicked him in the balls, Charlie thought. But that wasn't going to hold him at bay long. He stood up, ready to attack again. Charlie shouted clumsily, "Get the

fuck away from her!" It wasn't much of a threat, but it distracted the guy long enough to turn him away from Leah and face Charlie. A drug-ravaged skeleton stared back at him. Hollow cheeks, sunken eyes, missing half an ear: every nightmare Charlie's mother had planted in his brain since he learned the phrase "stranger danger." Charlie wished he hadn't said anything at all. The monster turned heavily, clearly still hurting from the blow Leah had landed. But when he saw Charlie, the weight seemed to vanish, and he lunged. Charlie had just enough time to deflect the blow, but the second followed faster than he thought, and connected with his eye. A light burst in his head, but somehow he managed to keep his feet, even blocked the third blow, and pushed forward into the onslaught, swinging blindly, scraping his knuckles on flesh and bone and rock.

Somewhere, he heard Leah shouting for someone to stop. Him? The other guy? He couldn't tell. Then she was joining the fight, wrapping her arm around the guy's throat while Charlie beat his face and gut. Grunting, but refusing to drop, he twisted and turned, trying to fling the girl off his back. Somehow, Charlie ended up side to side with Leah, and he felt the bulge of the knife in her belt. Why hadn't she used it?

He reached inside her coat and grabbed the knife. It slid out faster than he expected, and he almost cut her. But she knew what was happening, and let go. She dodged out of the way while Charlie drove the blade into the attacker's side. It slid smoothly, catching once on something that popped and gave way. Charlie couldn't tell how deep it went, but pushed harder just in case. He felt warm spurts of blood coating his hand, drenching his shirt. He heaved one more time, and the guy staggered away from them, dumbfounded, and slumped to the ground. He stared into the darkness, and Charlie stared back. There was no mistaking the eternity in his eyes. Charlie held the knife like a live thing, barely aware of what he'd done.

Finally, Leah slapped his face and grabbed him by the shoulder, "Let's go, she said. "Now!" She took the knife and they scrambled back into the car. Charlie was putting it into gear before their doors were shut, and he bounced over the curb into the street.

After they'd gone two or three blocks, she told him, "Slow down. We don't want to be stopped for speeding."

"He could be after us. He knows who you are."

"He doesn't know anything anymore, Charlie."

"What happened?" He let his foot up off the gas, but he still felt they were flying at a thousand miles an hour.

"The son of a whore got greedy," she said. "Pull up over there." She pointed at an apartment complex. Behind it, they found a dumpster, and she buried her coat in the garbage. Then she dropped the knife down a sewer grate. Back on the road, Charlie felt a little safer, but his hands were still sticky with blood.

"What'll your mother say about the jewelry?"

"Nothing. She's gone."

"Like. . . dead?"

Leah laughed. "Yeah, like dead. Except she's alive and well and ignoring the three of us. That's why my father sits there with the gun. I think he'll kill her if she ever decides to come back."

"So you use the money to. . ."

"Not to get high. I figure she left me a nest egg. By the way, you're speeding again. Turn into those woods there."

Automatically, Charlie followed her instructions. He drove as far as the trees would let him and killed the engine. The sudden darkness was complete.

"Open the trunk. Let's see what we got," Leah said.

He popped the trunk and they rummaged through it until Leah found a plastic tool case and a length of hose.

"This will have to do." She dumped the tool kit and left it open on the ground. Then she lifted the fuel tank door and unscrewed the cap. Charlie watched uncomprehending until she stuck the hose in and started sucking. When the flow started, she let the gas pour into the tool case until it was full, and then crimped the hose. "Splash it inside. Leave your phone, too."

The voice spoke up to tell him no, don't listen to that crazy girl, but then it fell into irrelevant silence. He sloshed the gas along the back seat and came back for more. After two more trips, Leah took a lighter from her pocket. "Your shirt, too," she told him.

He pulled it over his head, glad he still wore a ratty T under it. Shivering, he threw the bloody shirt inside. The smell of gas hovered like a toxic fog everywhere, while the last of it dripped to the ground from the hose in the tank.

"Stand back." She clicked the lighter, and threw it flaming into the front seat. It landed on the shirt, and instantly the interior was blazing with sooty heat. The last thing Charlie saw was his swim bag melting into a pool of nylon gunk.

The heat pushed them back, but they stood watching the inferno. His mind briefly registered her hand in his.

"It's long walk home," Charlie said finally. "We better get started."

The flames threw their shadows toward the road ahead of them, flickering and alive.

◇◇◇◇◇◇

Lavina

Richard Prosch

◇◇◇◇◇◇

Lavina was short, with a peaked face and a wild mane of salt and pepper hair best described as frizzy. The kind of woman Danny Parks never would've noticed even though she lived two doors down, sharing his townhouse building.

The place had four two-story units. Danny and his girlfriend Tammy lived on one end, Lavina and her whatever-he-was on the other.

Lavina's live-in was too young to be her husband, said Tammy, picking at her cranberry salad, twirling the lettuce around on her fork.

"I 'm still not sure who you're talking about," said Danny, pouring another glass of Vignoles.

"The woman in the end apartment. The one looks like Rhea Perlman."

"Who?"

"Rhea Perlman on Taxi." Tammy giggled. "She sorta looks like Ronnie James Dio. You know, the heavy metal guy?"

"Oh yeah," Danny got the Dio reference. "I saw her at the mailboxes the other day." He emptied half his glass. "Are you eating that salad or making and origami duck?"

"So do you think the big guy is her son, or boyfriend, or what?

Danny threw back the rest of the wine and didn't bother to wipe his lips. "Who cares?"

"I think she's a spook," said Tammy.

Two days later Danny came home to one less neighbor. Before he'd even put his Ford Escort into park, he saw the open door on the unit next to Lavina's.

Bob, the apartment manager, greeted him on the sidewalk. "Looks like you're losing a neighbor," he said.

"Elderly couple wasn't it? What's going on?"

"Mr. and Mrs. Peterson. Apparently she up and walked away a couple nights back."

"I didn't know she was having trouble. Dementia?"

"Not that I knew about."

Danny's stomach tightened with the look on Bob's face.

Oh, no.

Bob nodded as if he could read Danny's mind. "They found her this morning up in the woods. Been dead a while too. Looks like some stray dogs got to her."

"I guess I could've gone without hearing that."

"Just saying." Bob snuffed hard and spit into the parking lot. "The old man's gone to stay with his kids. Wanted me to water the plants, keep an eye on things until they could make arrangements to move."

By the time supper rolled around, Danny was starved, but Tammy wouldn't eat.

"I just keep thinking about that poor old woman. Laying up there. Dogs."

"It happens. Pass the ketchup, please?"

"You know what? I wonder if that Lavina had anything to do with it."

"How could she?"

"Bob told me that the Peterson's had complained about her. About her arguing with her boyfriend. Or whoever he is."

"I saw the guy you mean. Big, bearded skinhead guy out polishing the wheels on his car." Danny described the big man and his tattoo sleeve arms.

"That's him," said Tammy.

"If you're worried about anybody," said Danny, "worry about him. He's a hell of a lot more scary than Lavina."

"I think they're both scary."

"Have a glass of wine."

Two weeks later, another neighbor was gone. Dan and Tammy had been on a weekend outing to the mountains. When they returned, Bob was sweeping the sidewalk outside of a yellow tape barrier. The tape read CRIME SCENE in big black letters.

"Damnedest thing," said Bob when Danny asked him about it. "Nobody heard a thing. I didn't even know Jerry was home."

Jerry drove a truck on long hauls up the coast. He was often gone for weeks at a time. Sharing the apartment wall with quiet, absent Jerry was one of the things Danny appreciated about his apartment.

Now Jerry was absent for good.

Bob jerked his thumb toward the sealed apartment. "Lot of blood in there."

That night neither Danny nor Tammy ate supper.

A month later, after they'd answered a few routine questions for the cops and most of the excitement was over, Tammy mentioned seeing Lavina at the mailbox. "She was really shook up about something. Real jittery." She could've been talking about herself. "Danny, I think her arms were bruised."

An image of the skinhead in all his inked glory popped into Danny's mind. "You think that bastard's hitting her?"

"Remember the Petersons complained about their arguing?"

"That sonuvabitch," said Danny. Compared to an unsolved murder next door, old-fashioned domestic violence seemed fairly routine. It seemed like something a neighbor could do something about.

"Next time you see Lavina," said Danny. "Invite her in for coffee."

It happened sooner than Danny would've predicted.

Two nights later, when the knock came at the door, they both jumped.

Danny cracked open the door, keeping the security chain firmly in place. In the darkness outside, by the glow of the parking lot lights, Lavina stood, shrunken, sullen, blood on her sweatshirt. Blood on her face.

"Can I use your phone?" Meek. Crying.

If the sight of blood trickling out of Lavin's nose didn't immediately jerk Danny's insides into a knot, the shadow of the skinhead did. He stood back a ways, behind Lavina, close to Dan's car. His legs shoulder-width apart, his arms loose by his sides.

Then Tammy was there at the door, unhooking the chain, swinging the door wide to let Lavina in.

The woman's eyes were wide, begging for help. "Come in," said Tammy. "I'll get my phone."

As Danny turned to close the door, the skinhead spoke to him.

"What was that?" said Danny. He had to strain his ears to hear.

"Send the bitch back out."

Oh, yeah. Right.

"So she can take another beating? Is that it? You haven't had enough fun?"

Seeing Lavina the way she was had fired up something inside Danny. Two deaths in the same building. Now this creep working over a helpless woman.

Danny threw caution to the wind and stepped outside, closing the apartment door behind him.

By now, Tammy would be getting Lavina some help. Cleaning her up. Making some calls.

"This has to stop, man," said Danny, walking forward. "You can't just—"

The skinhead staggered forward. There was blood on him too.

"Send her out," he said. "Or she'll...she'll hurt you too."

The big guy fell over in a pile on the sidewalk.

Tammy?

Danny spun, rushed back to the door.

It was locked from inside.

◇◇◇◇◇

St. Girard's Ink Den

Mark Rapacz

◇◇◇◇◇◇

I woke up at noon because it sounded like there was a cat-fight in my yard. I went outside and instead there was a raccoon biting its tail. I didn't know what to do. The sun was hot, and I was still sweating from a restless sleep. The raccoon was sick. Likely rabies. It foamed at the mouth and gnawed on its tail. It sounded like it was hacking something up, but at the same time it shrieked like a dying cat. It retched a bloody mess onto my driveway. I realized I was watching for a little too long, but my neighbor came up to me and said he could shoot it with a pistol he had. He was always looking to help since I cleaned his gutters last spring. I said, no, I'll take care of it.

By the time I grabbed my shovel, a group of neighborhood kids had gathered in my yard. I swung and stabbed at the animal's neck. I chopped down, again and again, and the resilience of its neck muscles was surprising. It shook its head back and forth, growled, and foamy mucus flew from its mouth. I kept hacking and I wanted the kids to turn away. My neighbor grabbed a bat and hit it in the side, but his swings only agitated the animal. Finally, as the sweat beaded off my forehead and dripped onto the little beast, its legs started twitching, and then it died. I buried it in my garden, and went back to bed.

Lying in the still sweat-soaked sheets, I rolled over to wake up Megan to tell her what happened. She pretended to sleep. It was twelve forty-five. I would get up at one o'clock and make some coffee. I would pour Megan a cup and make her breakfast, but she wouldn't eat it. I would keep pouring her coffee, and I would tell her all about the raccoon, but she would just read the paper. We would stumble around until two o'clock when I would go to the parlor, and she would head off to work as a waitress. She would tell me she hates her boss, and that she needs a new job. I would agree with her. We would kiss each other goodbye and then we would tell each other we would miss one another. I would spend all day inking other people's flesh, and then I would come home and be with Megan again, and we'd go to sleep. I would wake up the next day at one o'clock and then make breakfast.

◇◇◇◇◇◇

I owned the oldest Tattoo parlor in the Bay Area, or so it said on our neon sign that didn't work—St. Girard's Ink Den, Oldest Tattoo Parlor in the Bay Area—but it was nowhere near the oldest. It was a burrito shop when I ended up on this coast twenty years ago. My shop attracted the younger crowd who got tattoos that didn't mean shit. They'd be kids coming in after finals or after humping in a dorm room, wanting to put a name on their arm, or on their pelvic bone.

Between appointments, I'd work on my paintings. I never thought they were any good, but some artsy kid from university said they were something else, and he bought one. It was a dragon eating a blood-filled egg. The kid said there's a market for this type of work.

◇◇◇◇◇◇

He also told me another time, "You have some natural skills," after I finished up a chintzy Chinese symbol. I didn't know what it said. The book translated it into meaning something like, "luck," "providence," or "god;" something like that. For all I know it could mean "sausage," or likely, "idiot" for getting such a cheap tattoo. Although the kid wasn't referring to his arm, he was pointing at a pencil sketch I did of a skeleton princess. She had bones for a body, and a rotten fleshy head, but I did my best to make her look beautiful. The kid went on and said I reminded him of an artist that started with an S. He asked if I knew the guy, or had seen the guy's work. I said the only work I see is in my head or in these tattoo books.

I ran into the same kid, one late night, when I was heading to my car and walking by one of the college bars. He looked at me, and he was obviously drunk, but he wanted to talk. He was average-sized and good-looking too. He wore all black. Smart kid. He said he wanted another tattoo and wondered if I had the time to do it right then and there. It was a bone cross. Terrible, but he had done it himself on a bar napkin. I don't ink drunken kids, so I told him he should keep the design and look it over tomorrow to decide if he'd want it. He looked off into the distance and started saying a lot of stuff about art and inspiration, the way that type does when they've had too much to drink. Then he looked at me.

"Where are you from? Chicago?"

"Never been, where you from?"

"No, I mean what school did you go to? NYU, LA? What?"

I'm a disheveled guy, wild hair, wild beard, ratty clothes, but I've never been mistaken for an artist before. I looked at the kid like I was his parent and I said, "Wouldn't you like to know." He smiled like he

knew something, and I smiled like I knew what it was he knew, but I didn't. "Later, man," I said, and I kept walking.

◇◇◇◇◇◇

Megan left me a burger and fries from the restaurant in the fridge. The ketchup on the burger reminded me of the raccoon remnants so I couldn't eat it. I poured myself a 49ers souvenir cup of whisky and tea over ice and sat on the front step. It was late and Megan was already in bed. I watched the sporadic traffic drive by and the brown clouds skirt around the moon. Across the street my neighbor was watching television. He never slept. I wanted it to rain. I drifted in and out of a surreal buzz from the booze with thoughts of Megan sleeping alone in my room.

Megan used to cut herself. I never actually saw her do it. Not once. She could have been over it, I don't know. I tried not to spend much time looking at the scars. They were there, but she was too, and that was the important part. I met her at my shop. She wanted a tattoo, one of those tattoos that chicks get these days, the kind of Asian or Mediter-ranean thing at the small of their backs. I talked her out of the tattoo. I've seen tattoo fads come and go, and I didn't want to mess up her perfect back.

"Man with the style of a hippie with a biker prob-lem gives me advice?" was what she said.

"You don't need to listen to me. You just have a nice back. Don't want to ruin it." I didn't know if that was inappropriate.

Then she asked with a glint in her eye, "Really?"

We settled on a butterfly near her navel. Classic. As my needle approached she got this look in her eye. It was excitement and pleasure wrapped into one like

TOUGH

the countless yin-yang tattoos I've inked on a lot of stranger's bodies.

When I finished, she came out of a sort of trance and sat up.

The first thing she said, was "My boyfriend is such a cocksucker."

Surprised, I tried to listen to all the pains this cocksucker had put her through—and they were many—but I was also more interested in dressing her tattoo. Before I knew it, I said, "What kind of cocksucker wouldn't love you?"

She laughed. It was a fake laugh. "You don't know him."

Then she started to cry. She was distant and a mess, so of course she found me. I hugged her because I thought that was what she wanted. She didn't hug back. She asked me to take her somewhere safe, so I made the mistake of bringing her home, and we didn't do anything. She slept two days straight.

Back on my step, focusing on my neighbor's television late at night with Megan still asleep, I thought of her past, and I thought of her as someone's kid. She wasn't too much older than the university kids, and I'm much older than that. Inappropriate, most likely. I went back in and topped off my 49ers cup to show them how big of a fan I am and went to bed and lay next to Megan. Her eyes were shut and drool was crusting on her smooth cheek.

"I think I need another tattoo, babe," she mumbled. "Could we go soon?"

◇◇◇◇◇◇

It was another week and it was full of Chinese kanji, barbed-wire armbands, and wiggly things that people drew themselves. People get tattoos with no meaning attached to them. Tattoos should mean something, it is a brand, and it is personal, and you sure as shit better want it on you for the rest of your life. These kids don't imagine what their tattoo will look like when their skin goes soft and saggy, when the ink will fade and lines will blur. They don't know their armband will look like a blue smudge years from now, and what did it mean?

◇◇◇◇◇◇

Still, I tell every customer that it looks great. They all leave happy.

A girl with a black eye came in with her bull-dog-looking boyfriend, and he paid for her to get a tattoo high up on her inner thigh that said Chacho. I noticed she already had another name on her other inner thigh that said Nathaniel. I wondered who gave her the black eye, and then I told them to have a nice day as she walked out bow-legged.

The arty kid came back, and he had his bar napkin with the bone cross, but he didn't want to talk about the tattoo. He wanted to talk art, so he reached into his backpack and handed me a book about an artist whose name I couldn't pronounce. He told me to really look at pages 56 through 79 because they were his later works, and they reminded him of my work. He even told me some titles. Real dark shit. The kid was right. I did appreciate it. Then we talked more about art, inspiration, all that shit I hated, but with the kid it was all right. I let the kid roll himself a joint as he spoke endlessly about his professors and what they would tell him and how they're all posers and dumbfucks. He offered me a drag. I told him I stayed away from the stuff.

"You do anything else?" he asked, like I'd be interested.

"What do you mean?"

"Like, other shit man. You know what I mean."

"I do whisky."

He looked at me—condescending. Disappointed that I no longer did other shit, whatever he meant by that. I called him on it.

"What do you got?"

"What do you want?"

"It's not rocket science to get a prescription out here."

"I'm not talking about weed. I can get everything else." He chuckled, and he looked quick to my arms to tell me that he knew I knew he saw the few dimes of shiny scar tissue on my arms.

"Ah, I see," I said. "You want a better look," and I put my arm under the light so we could see a history I had intended to forget. "The skin is dead there from abscesses. Pretty cool, huh?" I said because the kid wanted me to impress him.

He was delighted. "That is what I'm talking about. Things are different now, though. Smoother kick—no needle. No spoon. No—" he waved his hand to dismiss my scars like they were nothing but pinpricks. "Whatever you junkies did in your day," he said.

I took my arm from the light and we sat in that silence as if we were waiting for something to break. Maybe it did.

"Pills, man," he finally said. "We're flooded. If you want pills, I got pills for you. All I'm saying."

I leaned back in my chair and thought about the many ways I would like to dismember the kid. I thought about my shovel and the raccoon and its shallow grave in my garden.

"Sounds a little weak for me," I said to further delight this kid and see how far he wanted to take the mystery I was creating for myself—for him.

He reached into his backpack and pulled out a prescription bottle. He shook it seductively as if he were jerking it or me off.

"People like it," the dumb braggart said.

"I'm sure they do," I said and he understood what I was saying and he graciously didn't push it any further. He put the bottle in his pack and changed the subject back to art and the meaning of the squiggly mess upon his forearm. It took me a moment to realize it was supposed to be the bone cross on the bar napkin.

"I told you to wait on that," I said.

"I was drunk."

"They're not supposed to ink when the client's drunk. Illegal."

"She was drunk, too," he chuckled and wanted me to laugh with him. I didn't.

"Think you can clean this up?" he asked.

"I can," I said.

◇◇◇◇◇◇

The first day Megan had off, we went to the shop. She wanted another tattoo and she had this idea. She always just tells me her ideas, and then I do them with as much care as I can. She has me do a tattoo when she's not feeling right, when things are down, when she's itchy. I know she needs one when she starts scratching her scars. She scratches until they bleed, and I ask her why, and she says because it's easier to do it than to not do it. I try to understand it and tell myself that I do. I don't.

She gets in her zone. She's on my bench, and I am touching her, and I am inking her, but she's not there. She's not in the room. I hear her breaths, and slight wince of pain. I read somewhere that there's a chemical that's released in the blood stream when consistent pain is administered; it has a numbing effect like opium. Her toes are now the heads of her favorite birds, and her left foot is a wooded path up a mountain, while her right is a radiant sun either rising or setting over the sea. Both legs are full of mythical creatures, and dying things. Things are decaying, birthing, and some are being reborn. There's a phoenix on her hip and an elephant trunk down her forearm that covers many of her scars. Her ears have tattooed earrings, and on the back of her neck there are four dots that are symbolic of something in another country. Her back is becoming my masterpiece. When things get bad, we work on her back. I finish, and she comes back to me. "Did you hear the rain?"

"That was the faucet," I said.

"What?"

"I was washing my hands."

⬦⬦⬦⬦⬦⬦

A couple weeks later the kid was back in the shop with another sketch. He wanted it on his arm, up on the shoulder, where a lot of men get their most important tattoos. His was of a Christ-like figure being crucified on a swastika. Another cross. Kind of. He said it says something about society. When I finished it, I told him it was great and that I really dug the vivid imagery, like I really saw what he was going for. He explained a lot about what the piece did for him and what it said about everything and it all sounded like bullshit.

"So you're the artist. You do all the tattoos, do you have any?" he said as he lingered with his backpack. If he opened it again, I planned to deck him in the mouth.

I only had one, and I never show anyone. It's on the top of my pelvic bone. It's a little butterfly with a flower near it. There's a looping dotted line following the butterfly, symbolizing its flutter. The butterfly is headed toward the flower to drink its nectar. I thought it was really pretty. It's hard to see with all the gray hair that has started to grow around it. I've begun to call them weeds in my flower garden.

He laughed hysterically.

"The master of tattoos has that? You must've been high when you got it. Tell me you were high." This coming from a kid with a swastika tattooed to his arm.

"I wasn't."

"Why don't you just remove it?"

"Right," I started to put my equipment away. "Never thought of that."

"Just get rid of it. I'll help you with a new one, you know, something that says something, not that blah." Then he stuck a finger in his mouth, fake retching.

"I'm fine with it," I said.

Then Megan walked in with our lunch. She was always good at reminding me that I needed to eat. She didn't come straight over to see me, which was odd. The kid quit being so gabby, and everyone stared at each other like they do when the air gets thick and tense. I turned to the kid, and I said, "I'd like you to meet Megan. She's one of my best customers." Sometimes she gets uncomfortable when I tell people we're seeing each other because of our age difference.

The kid quickly got up, pulled his sleeve down and said, "Good to see you, Megan."

"Yeah. Nice to see you, too, Chris," she said.

I never knew the kid's name was Chris.

I looked at them confused and thought the old man thought of how kids these days just somehow know each other from the internet and their Snapchat.

Kids. Just fucking kids.

◇◇◇◇◇◇

Megan gave me some story about meeting the kid at a party somewhere after her shift at the restaurant. I decided to believe her and I also decided to close early. Canceling my appointments relieved both of us. Forgiveness was something I learned and it was easiest to get there if you didn't ask too many questions.

We went to the Presidio and we had one of those picnics that people in love have where they sit in the sun, look at how blue the sky is, and say nice things to one another. We were both awkward. We weren't used to going out in public together in the daylight.

Megan kept asking if something was wrong because when she'd talk to me I didn't have much to say.

"Hey, how'd the day go, any really terrible tattoos that people wanted?—I mean beside that awful swastika Jesus crap Chris got."

I didn't like her saying the kid's name again.

"Nah, nothing beside the Nazi shit. But they're all pretty awful."

And then we didn't say anything beyond what we saw right in front of us and I tried to find comfort in our discomfort as we watched Frisbee players run around on the grass. She was sitting cross-legged and I had my head in her lap. She looked down at my face. She looked sad. She pinched my right ear lobe and asked sincerely what was wrong.

"Nothing. Is there anything wrong with you?"

I got up and started walking toward the top of the bluff that overlooked the Bay. I looked at the Golden Gate Bridge and sun on the water and wished I were back home in the woods, far from the coast. Megan stood next to me. She got hold of my hand, and when my forearm rubbed against hers, I could feel her raised and bumpy scars. I noticed the wind.

"You ain't cold?" I said.

There was a silence, and then a pause. "Not really. They should've called this the windy city, right?"

"Chicago must've had it first."

"What's Chicago like?"

"Big, populated, windy, kind of like this, but shittier."

"Why don't you tell me stories like you used to? You're being quiet. What's wrong with you, old man?"

"You know I was married before?"

Megan said, "No shit. You've told me about a dozen times."

I knew I had told her before, but I had to make sure, so I said, "So you know how it ended and everything."

She didn't say anything I just felt her head nuzzle into my neck.

"I showed that kid my tattoo. He laughed."

"Oh, babe," she said and she stretched her arms around my body and laid her head into the pit of my arm. "Chris is a fucking asshole."

◇◇◇◇◇◇

My back hurt from leaning over this large drag queen all afternoon who wanted a tattoo the length of her spine. Painful for the both of us, and worse in the heat. An impossible wave of humid stink settled over the city and the Bay wasn't taking any of it out to sea. People were all trying to stay cool and that meant business was slow. I closed the shop early and headed home.

◇◇◇◇◇◇

When I got home, heat lines rose out of the tar in my driveway. I went into the house and opened all of the windows. I never realized how much of a mess my house was. I determined right then and there I would clean it and get things organized. It was time for a change. I didn't expect Megan home till her shift was done around two, so I thought it'd be a nice surprise her if there weren't dirty dishes in the sink and our bedroom had clothes that were folded.

For extra motivation, I first went to the kitchen and filled a souvenir cup to the brim with tea and whisky and organized my thoughts in the heat on my step. I decided maybe it was time Megan and I hit the road. San Francisco wasn't good for her. Our future was north in Seattle, or maybe even further into Canada. I didn't know for sure. The sky was yellowy dust. It looked like it so painfully wanted to be a nice clear day that it was stressing itself out. My feet ached. I looked at my truck. It had gone 200,000 miles too far. I started doing economics in my head. It was going to work out, I was sure of that.

When I went back into the house, I decided the bedroom was where I'd start. Megan spent most of her time in there, so I'd spend most of my time making it look good. The hallway had a peculiar cool dry feel to it and it felt dirty, because it was dirty, but dirtier than usual. It was in the air. Another thing I determined I'd somehow fix. I came to the door. It was only open a crack.

A morning light flooded the room even though it was five o'clock. Her foot with the bird tattoos hung off the bed. Megan lay there like a child. She looked nice, a young sort of nice, sleeping so peacefully in the mistaken dawn. I walked over to the bed and kissed her cold cheek. Her face was always cold, a circulation thing she'd say. She was sure to get shit from her boss at the restaurant for missing work like this. Like it mattered. We were leaving and she'd be happy to leave with me. I leaned down to kiss her again on her forehead. She was unmoved, oblivious. The bedspread was tangled a bit, so I adjusted it to tuck her in. When I pulled back the spread there it was: a pill bottle. Possibly Chris's pill bottle. It looked like a trinket that should be atop an old woman's piano. It was terrifying in its normality.

I could've dragged her to the garden and buried her with the raccoon. But she breathed like a child. Slept like a child. She was a child. I was, too.

I checked her pulse, her temperature—as I had done for others—and then tucked her in. I pocketed the bottle to talk about it later and kissed her again.

I ended up outside on my step for I don't know how long. The sky was closer. Trees that I've seen thousands of times were misshapen. Houses that once stood straight and tall now looked parabolic. It was dark by the time I left.

◇◇◇◇◇◇

I spent the night in the shop. Not sleeping. Waiting mostly. I waited for dawn, pacing and watching for real living people to pass in front of my parlor. I kept all of the lights on and stared out the window. I could see my whole shop in the reflection: the barber shop chair that I liked to use for arm tattoos, the massage bench I liked to use for back tattoos, the same bench where I met Megan. There was my counter, my dentist table with needles and dyes on it, my crumpled handkerchief, and the over-head light. I could see some of my paintings shoved in the corner. I hoped the sun would come up soon.

◇◇◇◇◇◇

I stayed up as long as there were fingers left in the bottom of my bottle. I was expecting a call from Megan, but I really had no idea how long she'd be out. I started to get anxious, like I did something wrong. I was paranoid, weak, sullen and drunk. I couldn't stop fidgeting, so I called her, multiple times, but there was no answer. Near dawn I passed out.

I woke up to fists hitting my store window and a silhouette of a person at my door. For a moment, I thought Megan, but then I came to my senses. This person's hands were big and ham-fisted and there were others with him. He started to pound again.

I struggled out of my chair and I felt my age course down my legs. I was no longer drunk. At the door, my stomach dropped. Cops. I didn't want to know, but I already knew because the past is the real cocksucker.

After I did my best to convince them I had nothing to do with it; after I said I thought she was recovering and that I didn't supply her the pills; after I said I had checked on her—really checked on her; after I said she seemed not OK, but OK for what she'd done; after I told them that I didn't have any family in the city and she didn't either; after I told them for tenth time I didn't know why I said she was my wife because I meant girlfriend; after I told them I didn't run and I wasn't fucking hiding; after I said of course I knew my neighbor and it was not unusual he stopped by in the middle of the night; after I told them to leave and assured them I wouldn't run because I was of course going to fucking go to the coroner's—

After all this and other things I cannot remember, I went back to my stool. I sat like a statue in my shop that felt narrower, with a ceiling that was lower, and surrounded by needles that were larger than I remembered.

I prepared my kit, swabbed my arm and waited for that gentle whir when the needle would track my flesh.

◇◇◇◇◇◇

Detour

Tom Andes

◇◇◇◇◇◇

As the plane circled New Orleans, Kachenko looked at his watch. They'd left Dallas an hour and twenty minutes late. He sipped the last of his bloody mary mix, rattling the cubes in the plastic cup.

He saw Jonas at baggage claim. At least he felt reasonably certain it was Jonas; years had passed since he'd seen the other man, and then Kachenko had encountered Jonas in a professional setting, also. Kachenko's garment bag depending from one shoulder, the small attaché case with his personal effects dangling at his side, he brushed past a person who strongly resembled Jonas, at any rate, and who broke a grin and raised his white hat as he passed Kachenko and hurried outside. Waiting for the shuttle to the rental car center, Kachenko saw Jonas—or the man he took to be Jonas—at the cab stand a few hundred yards down the curb. With a hissing of air brakes, the shuttle arrived; at almost exactly the same instant, the white hat disappeared inside a yellow cab, and the race was on.

On the shuttle, Kachenko opened his flip phone. His contacts were empty. He dialed the number from memory.

"Yes?" the voice answered, with a touch of the familiar impatience.

"He's here." Kachenko's voice betrayed only a trace of an accent.

"Who's there?"

"Jonas," Kachenko said.

"Are you sure of it?" the voice asked him, after a silence.

Kachenko considered the question. Was he certain? He thought of the white hat, the broad grin, the clear expression of recognition…"Yes," he said.

"Very well," the voice said, and the person on the other end of the phone sighed. "You know what this means, and you know what you have to do."

Kachenko closed the phone. He held it in his fist for the duration of the ride, watching the lights on the runway in the distance as the shuttle trundled along the access road.

The kid behind the Hertz desk told him he'd been upgraded, free of charge, and led Kachenko across the lot to a gray Suburban. Kachenko tossed his garment bag in back; he set the attaché case on the passenger's seat. He found the pistol attached to the underside of the dashboard with packing tape, just as his instructions had promised it would be, along with a silencer and two extra magazines, and he screwed the silencer onto the pistol and checked to be sure the pistol was loaded before he started the vehicle. Opening his notebook, he punched the second of the two sets of coordinates he'd written down before he left Los Angeles into the GPS; he'd already determined he would have no time to go to his hotel.

On the highway, halfway between Kenner, the suburb where the airport was located, and the city itself, there'd been an accident. All five lanes on the interstate had backed up, and red brake lights irradiated the night, filling the windshield with a spectral glow. Gripping the wheel, Kachenko scanned the backs of the cars in front of him until he thought he saw that familiar white hat through the rear window of a yellow cab several car lengths ahead of him in one of the passing lanes, though he couldn't be certain, as the cab's window was filthy.

Traffic progressed at something less than a crawl. Like the spine of some antediluvian creature raising itself from the primordial muck, the highway stretched ahead of him, eastbound traffic retarded to a trickle while oncoming traffic streamed past, headlights glaring in the darkness. Kachenko consulted his GPS. Alongside the highway, the flashing red and yellow lights on the rescue vehicles played across the surface of a canal.

At the next exit, Kachenko signaled, and he nosed across two lanes and turned onto Veteran's Boulevard. Driving through the suburbs, he observed the speed limit. Box stores, plaza malls, and family restaurant chains flanked the dual carriageway; cross streets disappeared into darkness. Traversing another canal, he entered New Orleans: on his right was the Office of Motor Vehicles, a gray monstrosity of a building rising like a tombstone into the night.

Here, his GPS seemed to have abandoned him. He found himself navigating a subdivision, crooked paving blocks jutting from the roadway. The SUV bounced over the seams between the blocks; twice, the Suburban bottomed out, its brakes grating as they locked.

"Son of a bitch." Kachenko smacked the wheel.

He'd come to a dead end. On the other side of a cyclone fence, a railroad trestle drew a faint charcoal line through the darkness; behind him, the residential homes with their pristine lawns and carefully tended hedges seemed to have been dropped into that devastated landscape from some other part of the world, perhaps from someplace where disaster didn't seem quite so imminent. Kachenko threw the truck into reverse, and he nearly backed into a garbage can as the Suburban bounced in and out of a massive pothole, or maybe it was a sinkhole, Christ, Kachenko wondering he hadn't snapped an axle.

As he turned, his headlights swept a DETOUR sign with an arrow pointing to the left.

Kachenko signaled—one had to retain some sense of order in the midst of so much chaos, after all—and he piloted the SUV onto an empty boulevard named for some dead French king (one of the Louies, he would remember later). After he'd gone three blocks, he understood this detour would be interminable: though he scanned the near distance for another orange sign that would point him back to the path he'd been on, setting him on the way to downtown New Orleans, he knew he would never find it.

He pulled to the curb, and he punched the same set of coordinates into the GPS. Orange barrels marked the periphery of the construction zone; he had to drive the wrong way down a one-way street to escape the subdivision. Recalibrating, the GPS repeated in a bland voice that nevertheless seemed to excoriate him for having failed to obey its directive. Signaling, he turned, and he drove toward the center of the city at exactly five miles per hour over the speed limit; under the streetlights, he glanced at the gun on the seat beside him.

He parked several blocks down the street from the hotel and convention center on Poydras, which was clogged with yellow cabs. Stuffing the gun in his trousers, he adjusted his suit coat to cover it, and he locked the Suburban, which chirped, flashing its lights. The Wyndham rose from Poydras in a pillar of light. Approaching on foot, Kachenko thought he saw that familiar white hat enter the hotel between the marble columns, though he couldn't be certain.

Inside, the concierge, a bald-headed man of about fifty, asked if he could take Kachenko's bags.

"I don't have any bags," Kachenko said, his eyes scanning the crowd over the other man's shoulder for that white hat, trying to glimpse the banquet hall through the massive doorway at the other end of the lobby.

"Perhaps I can help you in some other way, sir?" The concierge leaned closer, trying to catch Kachenko's eye, barring his passage. "You are staying at this hotel, I presume?"

Kachenko fixed on the man's small black eyes. A hooked nose protruded from the concierge's face like a beak; he'd already reached the age where his ears and his nose had begun to outgrow the rest of his face. Though he stood several inches taller than Kachenko, they had roughly the same build.

"Yes, please," Kachenko said, wringing his hands. "I only meant I needed your help. Come this way, please..."

Stooped, bent—in spite of himself, intrigued—the concierge followed. In the hallway outside the men's room, with the other man close on his heels, Kachenko stopped, turned, and drove his elbow into the concierge's windpipe. The concierge's larynx cracked; staggering, he grabbed his neck, his face purpling as he drew a wheezing breath. Before he could fall to the floor, Kachenko caught the concierge around the waist, and Kachenko dragged the concierge into the bathroom, locking the door behind him.

In the handicapped stall, Kachenko snapped the other man's neck, and he propped the concierge up on the seat, removing his suit coat and his shirt. Where the clothing had fit the concierge loosely, hanging from his frame, it fit Kachenko snugly.

Yet it fit, Kachenko thought, shooting his wrists through the sleeves. Beneath his undershirt, the concierge's white skin looked like a turkey buzzard's, and Kachenko thought of his own childhood, that distant village: he experienced a patchwork recollection of children with tear-stained faces (had he been one of them?) kicking a soccer ball in the dirt and making way for the military vehicles rolling through. He didn't know where he'd come from, didn't know whether the memories were his or something he'd invented after seeing the evening news. Regardless, the years between then and now seemed a blank.

The concierge gave a last tremor of life, and his foot shot out, catching Kachenko's shin. Out of reflex, Kachenko punched the dead man in the face. He stared at the other man as though he'd come back to life; then, kneeling in front of the toilet, he began to remove the concierge's trousers.

"That son of a bitch isn't getting my money," he said. "He's not getting there first."

The words echoed in the empty bathroom.

His nose curled. The concierge had already voided his bowels.

He left the concierge on the toilet seat with a copy of the Baton Rouge Advocate he'd found on the tile in front of the baby changing station unfolded on his lap. He looked at himself in the mirror, squeezing a blackhead and splashing some water on his face before he left the room. Dressed in the top half of the concierge's uniform, Kachenko crossed the lobby at a brisk pace, whistling to himself as he walked. Chandeliers glittered beneath the ribbed vault of the ceiling. The room seemed to hold the voices of everyone in it, echoing, with an air of hushed expectation, like a concert hall before the symphony starts. In the dining room, Kachenko stood next to a tray of bread puddings, scanning the rows of pillars along the perimeter of the room for that white hat.

The candidate occupied a position of honor at the center of the room. Six foot one, hair graying at the temples, scion of some local political dynasty, he projected the kind of benevolent grandfatherly charm that might have appealed to a populist reformer at either end of the political spectrum, though whether he was running for president, councilman, alderman, city coroner, or for the school board, much less what his politics were, Kachenko didn't know; he only knew that in order to get paid, he had to finish the job, and he had to do it before Jonas did it. The white hat appeared on the other side of a pillar at the end of the banquet hall; then it disappeared again.

His hand on the butt of the pistol, which he'd stuffed in the pocket of his trousers, Kachenko crossed the room, weaving between a pair of waiters who followed him with their eyes. At the far end of the dining room, that white hat appeared between the pillars—and there, closer at hand, he thought he saw that same white hat on the other side of the room, and he didn't know how Jonas had moved so quickly. Blinking sweat from his eyes, teeth gritted, as he approached the candidate's table, he withdrew the pistol from his pocket, and he fired three shots at point-blank range into the candidate's heart. Muffled by the silencer, the pistol's reports sounded like a set of flapping wings. Kachenko knocked over the headwaiter, upsetting a dessert cart, scattering silverware across the floor. The candidate had risen halfway from his chair, as though he meant to shake Kachenko's hand; he pitched over backwards, blood spreading across the white ruffles of his shirt beneath the tuxedo jacket, blue eyes glazing as they rolled upward in his skull, as though he were gazing at the bandstand.

Silence fell over the room. Kachenko kept walking. He dropped the pistol in a tureen of crab and corn bisque on a buffet cart and proceeded at a calm but steadily accelerating pace toward the doors.

As he pushed the doors open, a woman—the candidate's wife—shrieked.

Kachenko emerged into a long hall decorated with Chinese lanterns. At the end of the hall, a doorway opened onto the street. As Kachenko walked the length of the hall, he brushed past a man in a white linen suit wearing a hat similar or perhaps identical to the hat Kachenko had seen Jonas wearing in the airport; he saw several other similarly attired men lurking along the periphery of the hall, but none of their faces cracked open in recognition; none of them seemed to notice him.

He stripped off the concierge's jacket as he descended the marble steps in front of the hotel and stuffed it in a garbage can by the curb.

Wearing his undershirt, he crossed the street, digging in his pockets for the keys to the Suburban. In the distance, a siren shrilled. Kachenko kept walking, and he didn't look back; he didn't want to know what was happening behind him.

◇◇◇◇◇◇

Kennick

Nelson Stanley

◇◇◇◇◇◇

"They picked on the wrong fucking Gyppo this time," roars the man my little cousin Nattie is to marry. I think about pointing out that, technically, he's Pavee, so some might argue he's not in the strictest sense of the word a Gyppo, but seeing as I've just got him out of bed and his eyes are rolling in two different directions and he's waving a shooter about his head, now is probably not the time. Despite the soft drizzle, sweat's sloughing off him like an ice cube melting in hot weather: I can still see white powder crusted around his nostrils. His gut hangs heavy and hairy over his belt, cinched to a degree he's not required since puberty.

"You might want to put on a shirt?"

"I'll put on no fucking shirt," and he pushes me out the way of the trailer door, goes wobbling across to where his Merc's parked in front of the lock-up.

Auntie Fiance is trying to shepherd the children inside a trailer but it's not every day you see a shirt-less man screaming his head off and waving what looks like Judge Dredd's gun about as he fails to operate his own car's door. At least, not first thing on a Saturday morning.

"Francie mate," I babble, backing away, "We've got a dentist's driveway to tarmac, the machinery's been butchered-"

"I shall be doing the fucking butchering!" He falls down on his arse in the mud.

"Well, yeah, but we've got a Bomag with all its hydraulics smashed, we've got a-"

"I shall rip that fucking Duchie cunt's head clean off," he bellows, scrabbling to his feet, "and I shall piss in the hole for luck."

"You might not need a shooter, if you're just gonna rip his head off, Francie mate," I say, getting ready to fling myself behind the thin aluminium of the trailer door, for all the good that'll do me. "I mean, accidents happen-"

"I'll fucking accident you, you fucking Kennick cunt," he screams, wheeling away from the seemingly impregnable door of his AMG. He waves the piece at me, or at least, in my general direction. "Come over here. I need a fucking driver, and you'll do as well as anyone else."

I struggle with the mental equivalent of a slipping clutch.

"I- I don't think I'd be insured, Francie," I manage. "German car interiors always make me feel sick, too. It's the smell of the upholstery-"

"Get in the car, hedge-mumping cunt." The awful hole in the end of that ridiculous gun swings toward me again. The Merc starts with a purr. I fiddle helplessly with the complicated foot-operated parking brake. "Get me to Duchie's, Kennick. And don't crash me fucking motor on the way, or I swear to Jesus, Mary and Joseph I'll spray your fucking brains all over this here car."

◇◇◇◇◇◇

I'd only gone down for my little cousin Emma-Louise's christening. In the church, Emma-Louise shit herself when raised up to the font. Nattie clung to my arm, burying her face in my shirt to stymie her laughter. We both agreed later that the clergyman had done well to make it to the end of the invocation. We all repaired to a pub to start the serious business of getting hideously drunk. While old men lined up to karaoke the standards of long-dead crooners, Aunt Kathy took me to one side.

"Kind of hoping you'd've got in there," she said.

"Eh? What? Me? With who?"

"Our Nattie." She regarded me seriously, as if over the top of a pair of glasses. She doesn't wear glasses.

"Nattie? B-but... She's me cousin!"

Aunt Kathy looked suitably horrified. After all, almost all of my relatives married someone they had a genetic relationship with: keep it in the family, like, or at least the tribe. My mother and father were, I think, second cousins. If that.

I grimaced, looked away around the room. Old men, supping pints. Small children dressed in posh but outdated Sunday best.

"Anything'd be better than the dinlo she's gone and got engaged to," said Aunt Kathy, sipping her gimlet and adjusting her hat.

"Who's that then, Auntie?"

She tilted her head and indicated the swollen bulk of Francie, swaying behind the mic, belting out "When You and I Were Young, Maggie" like half of Foster and Allen, if Foster or Allen weighed twenty stone and looked like they were smuggling breezeblocks strapped to their arms.

"Fat steroid boy on the mic?"

"He's a murderer," she muttered darkly.

"Say what?"

"Well. Accessory to. Held 'em down then buried the corpse, didn't he?"

"Jesus." I blinked. "Whatever happened to choring the wheels off of a vardo?" I asked. "When did we start playing proper gangsta?"

She shook her head sadly, took another pull on her gimlet.

"It's a wicked world, my sweet little chavvo."

◇◇◇◇◇◇

We drive. I think I do well, in the circumstances: I only stall the stupid overpowered car twice, and Francie doesn't blow my head off.

"I really love your fucking cousin," he says, when we slow down to negotiate a cattle-grid somewhere, fat low-profiles clump-thunking over the grate. I keep my head fixed front but my eyes slide sideways toward him. "I mean, I really love fucking her, too. But I also love the girl. She will make me a fine wife."

I pull up to the deserted little industrial estate, park outside Duchie's unit, which is on the end of the row of three, the one with the least number of smashed windows, conspicuously graffiti-free.

With his free hand he reaches across and pulls the electronic starter out of the dash, stuffs it into his trousers.

"You wait here, get me?"

Relief passes through me in a wave of warmth, a tingling dream of ecstasy strobing up from my toes to the crown of my head.

"Here? Right-o Francie, no problemo like—"

"This is an AMT Automag, Kennick. I got five shots. That gives me two spare. Don't do anything that'll lead me to wasting one of them on you, eh?"

I nod.

"Good." Out the corner of my eye I can see his gut heaving; the sweat pours off his chest and mats the wild hair in the deep valley of his pectorals. He gives my head a friendly push with the gun, then climbs unsteadily out of the car.

I watch him wobble across the buckling, weed-strewn car park. The breath goes out of me in a long stream. I cannot imagine how this day can get any worse.

A tapping, on the tinted window to my right.

One of Duchie's little helpers, Baz or Chris—I can't tell them apart—is leaning on the roof. He scrapes the barrel of the shooter he's been tapping the window with across my field of vision, makes motions I interpret to mean "Get out of the car." Outside, I shiver in the drizzle. His gun, I note with interest, is rather less compensatory than the one Francie was waving around, but is doubtless still big enough to ruin my life.

Ruin it some more, I mean. Out of sight, around the corner of the lock-up, I hear Francie scream.

◇◇◇◇◇◇

I ended up staying after the christening. Within a week I was out on the crew with Barry and Tommy and Vanni. Up at four, pile into a Transit van held together by rust and filler, drive to the arse-end of nowhere. Then ten, twelve hours laying asphalt.

"I'd let you on the mini-roller or the layer," said Barry, wiping a thick black smear across his sweating forehead, "But from the way you handle that rake I'd fear for me fucking life and for that of every other man on this site."

Then down the pub to drown whatever brain cells remained. It'd be digs in some flophouse if we were away on a job and when we worked closer to Francie's lock-up—upon which thirty or forty caravans were arrayed—Barry gave me the twins' old trailer to crash in. I'd collapse into sleep, hands shaking and numb from incipient nerve damage, burned all over and tired further down in my bones than I'd ever known possible. But it was good, it was good: family who I'd hurt and turned away from had opened their arms and welcomed me back, out of nothing more than the goodness of their hearts and my willingness to bend my neck over a shovel.

Tommy joked that Francie didn't like to get his hands dirty. He hawked a few cars on the side without bothering the taxman about it, via discreet adverts in the local paper. Every time he snaffled one up—part exchanges off dealer's forecourts, mostly—he'd send the motors out to Duchie's, and they came back waxed and buffed, primped and shining. Upon their return, each one went straight into Francie's lock-up, a task he was fanatical about seeing to himself. And every morning, no matter how he reeled, bleary-eyed, from the previous night's excesses, he'd have the van started and warmed up before we'd swallowed our paint-thick tea and bacon butties, and he'd hump the toolboxes out from the lock-up and stash them carefully in the back. Always sniffing, red-faced, wild-eyed, even in the driest weather.

"You watch the Kennick doesn't chore those toolboxes, Tommy," he'd chide us. Tommy would grin and nod and mug, but he made sure, I noted, to keep the keys to the padlock chained to him at all times, and when someone needed something he'd walk over himself to dole out the tools.

We were contracted for a month's work in Cardiff, on a big crew laying a new call-centre car park: Vanni shadow-boxing and boasting of the time when, as a boy, Uncle Cyril and Uncle Jack had taken him to see Howard Winstone lose to Vicente Saldivar for the undisputed world's title; up to Doncaster to do a private job on a man's farm, where Tommy regaled me with tales of the days when Uncle Charlie

and Uncle Durri would attend the races just after the war and Charlie once got into an argument with a man over a 10-1 shot and got a straight razor across his hip for his troubles.

I grew muscles I hadn't seen since I'd boxed and my "th"s all turned back into "F"s; I shaved more often and ate a lot of Joey Grey. I'd sit with the women, at a discreet, respectable difference from the men, and share a joke while the boys grumbled into their pints. Nattie would laugh with her head thrown back like a sword-swallower and chore roll-ups off me when she thought Aunt Kathy wasn't look-ing and I tried not to stare down her low-cut tops and stepped away when she moved close against me to whisper something conspiratorial that she didn't want the boys to hear, which was twenty times a day.

◇◇◇◇◇◇

We'd got up that drizzly Saturday morning and found someone had broken into Francie's lock-up during the night. We'd all been out on the piss even harder the night before, celebrating getting the cash-in-hand work to tarmac a local dentist's drive-way, a huge thing more autobahn than access route. He was going away for the weekend and wanted to return to find all the potholes turned into an asphalt billiard table.

I struggled out of bed to find Vanni, Tommy and Barry arrayed around the open door of the lock-up, wearing expressions you'd expect at a funeral. Someone had got in during the night. They'd jimmied the door, smashed the locks off the toolboxes, scat-tered tools all around the rough concrete floor; picks and shovels shattered, the mini-roller still on its trailer, sitting in a pool of hydraulic fluid, flaccid hoses hanging down like dead snakes. I set to helping Barry clean up: lots of stuff had been broken but weirdly nothing had been nicked.

"Gadjé bastards," said Barry, over and over, tears in his eyes. It wasn't just what it'd cost to fix the hoses, it meant we were down a roller, and that meant a day sorting another. "They'd burn us if they could get away with it!"

A crowd of relatives, near-relatives and assorted hangers-on had formed. No-one had seen anything, but everyone had an opinion that the next time some Gadjés from the local estate came calling, there'd be Hell to pay. Others counselled that we should move on—that, as ever, we had outstayed our welcome locally and should relocate.

"I can see the point in choring things," said Vanni, with what I thought a surprisingly philosophical tone, "but just smashing stuff up? Where's the sense in that?"

Tommy looked uncomfortable.

"Uh... I'm gonna go tell Francie that someone's knocked the shit out of his lock-up." He paused, big blue eyes fixed on me. "Actually, I'll go phone the man about his driveway, tell him we might be taking more time to finish than I thought. Why don't you go give Francie the good news, cuz? Cheer him up."

◇◇◇◇◇◇

I'm sat next to Francie. My front teeth have been knocked through my bottom lip, but apart from that I'm okay. I'm sitting on an old metal oil can, attached by a tow-chain you could moor a battlecruiser with to the Irish Traveller equivalent of Mechagodzilla and over in the corner Baz (or is it Chris?) is doing something to a big crowbar with what I assume to be an oxy-propane cutting torch. It fills the air with sparks and the reek of burning grease and hot metal and ozone, but I think it's just for show.

"Holy Mary mother of fuck, Duchie, there's no need for that shite," says Francie, who evidently doesn't believe that it's just for show. "I can tell you to the very ounce where your stuff's been going, like. If you was to have a word with my man Tommy-"

"Tommy?" I snap, "What's our Tommy got to do with this?"

"Shut up, Kennick," says Francie, squinting at me through purple swellings that render his eyes even more piggy-ish than usual.

"You sell out Tommy I'll fucking kill you myself," I snarl, spitting out blood. "Pavee piece of shit."

"Now now, boys. Inter-Gyppo racism is a terrible thing to behold." Duchie, a leathery Gadjé with something about him that reminds me of an ageing roadie for a heavy metal band, runs a hand through his greying mullet and grins a nasty gappy grin at me. "It's tearing apart your community. You'd think the oppressed could learn to all get along together, eh?"

"Traveller." I snap. "Inter-Traveller."

"Is it now? I don't know what you'd have to say about that, being a fucking Kennick of all things," mutters Francie, nearly lost in the spit and roar of the cutting torch.

One of Duchie's boys—whichever one isn't playing blacksmith over in the corner—lamps me around the back of the head. Francie has calmed down, but through the swellings and the drying blood glowers at Duchie with all the hate in the world.

"Got anything else to say, Francie?"

Francie holds his peace and flexes his shoulders, his huge meaty arms clanking the chain tight behind him, an action that drags me painfully to one side.

"That this morning wasn't nothing but a warning shot across your bows, Francie. You don't fuck about with me, I told you that." He shakes his head, a passable impression of a man gripped by a terrible and soul-deep sadness. "I know your lot's all in it together."

I start to say something and Baz or Chris steps around the front to punch me, having got bored of hitting me in the back.

"We're going to get all you boys in, eventually. One at a time. And we're going to sit each of you here and Chris over there-" the mush in the corner shuts off the cutting torch and turns around, the crowbar glowing before him in the gloom of the lock-up, smoke from his heavy welding gauntlets curling up into the air— "Is going to do to each of them what I'm about to get him to do to you, which is to ram this crowbar so far down your throat you'll be shitting sparks out your ringpiece like your arse was a fucking dragon."

From the look on Francie's face, I can only assume that Duchie is not the sort of fella who'd joke about this sort of thing.

"Then we'll get your little blonde piece in," continues Duchie, "And see what she's got to say about my missing fucking cocaine."

At the mention of Nattie I can't help it, a switch is flicked within me and I try and rise. Baz smashes me across the side of my face with the butt of his handgun.

I've been in a few decent street fights (and have run away from some really, really awesome ones). I've come off the back of a motorbike doing sixty round a bend and skidded for two hundred yards into a ditch, shredding my shoulder and busting my arm in two separate places. I've even had my heart broken a few times. Nothing I've ever done to myself or had done to me by an uncaring world has ever hurt quite so much as getting smashed in the face by that gun. I'm not sure if it's the heaviness of the thing, the oily hardness of it, or merely that it's just a terrible death-dealing device that should never be brought near a human being. It hurts like ffuck and I proceed to squeal and yammer in a most unbecoming way as the entire left-hand side of my face fills with blood.

Through the explosion going off behind my eyes and my brain pinging about the otherwise empty expanse of my skull, I see Duchie kind of put his forehead in his hand and massage his brow, like a man with a nasty headache coming on; I see Baz throw back his head to laugh, hands on hips and beergut wobbling below his stained Polo shirt; I see Chris pause and join in, smoke still pouring from his welding gauntlets. I see Francie slip his chains and rise from his oil can beside me with blood streaming from his wrists like a suicide whose just decided ending it all is a bad idea, after all.

No-one is more surprised, I think, than Baz when Francie cops hold of his shooter and wrenches it free and proceeds to use it to batter seven shades of shit out of him. The look of horror on Duchie's face is a wonder to behold.

Chris, to be fair, is made of sterner stuff, and swings the crowbar around with both hands, legs braced, like he's felling a tree. The glowing end of it comes around and when it hits Francie it does indeed make a bit of a mess of the man's shoulder. Despite the horrific sizzling noise and the smell—hideous, like when you drop your lit fag on the upholstery of a car crossed with the worst barbecue fuck-up ever, exploding proteins and boiling fat and skin—he seems to remember that the thing he's been using as a club can be employed in a more efficient manner, and he shoots Chris right through the forehead.

I've never heard a gun go off before. No-one ever told me that they were so shockingly, world-endingly loud. I'm suddenly thankful for all the damage I've already done to my hearing at bad hardcore concerts. Chris goes over backwards with half his head gone to bloody ruin.

Duchie pulls out Francie's gun from somewhere. I cannot possibly imagine where he's had it stashed. I'm impressed he can heft it without keeling slowly forward under the weight. Francie appears to weigh up his chances; then he smashes Baz in the mooey one last time with the gun then lets it drop to the floor.

Duchie says something I don't catch, what with the tinnitus and all, and he thumbs something on the gun I presume must be the safety. Then it strikes me that the chains that previously held me are slack after Francie managed to wriggle out of them and almost without conscious volition I lurch forward—chain and oil can and all—through the intervening space and hit Duchie as hard as I can on the side of the jaw. We go down in a tangle and behind the cold hard bite of the adrenaline something inside me is cowering, waiting for the explosion of light and pain that's going to end the one attempt in my entire miserable existence to play the hero, waiting for the bullet that'll rip through muscle and blood and bone and the fat links of the chain are oily and cold and slip in my hands as I bring them down again and again and again on Duchie's head and as my hearing comes back I think "Who's making that fucking high-pitched shrieking noise?" and I realise that it's me and by then Duchie's head is just so much blood and matted hair and with a shudder like coming inside someone

I love I finish and look up, nausea roiling against the earth-shattering world-ending pain in my head.

Francie is picking at the huge eschar—like a bad 90's tribal tattoo that's gone terribly wrong—on his shoulder, but he glances down and nods at me.

"That's not a bad job, for a Kennick," he says, conversationally, and I look at the blood on my hands and the bloody chain around me and my hands close on something else amongst the warmth of Duchie's corpse and I bring Francie's enormous handgun up, slowly, so slowly, it weighs a metric fuck-tonne, I've never felt anything so heavy but I bring it up steady and when I pull the trigger and shoot Francie right in the fucking face, he doesn't look a bit surprised.

◇◇◇◇◇◇

You've got to put your back into digging, much like you've got to put your back into life. Feel the heft against your muscles. Feel the strain on your spine. Feel the sweat sting your eyes, the bitumen sear in your mucus membranes. The roar of the roller is the background static that clouds out your life, makes you lose sight of what you want, both for yourself and the people you care about. Tonight, it is joined by the rattle and gravelly churn of a cement mixer, one Tommy borrowed off a mush who owed him a favour over a horse or a girl, I can't remember which.

Laying a driveway properly is best approached as a craft: a technical problem to be solved by the materials available. It is not usual to dig down an extra six feet and fill the resulting trench in with cement before packing over the top of it with hard-core and then layering on the asphalt; men like Barry or Vanni or Tommy would, in the general run of things, call you a fucking dinlo for even considering such a

thing, making such hard work out of a task that can be accomplished with much less effort.

This is not the general run of things. In this particular case it was needed, at least in Barry and Tommy's opinion, and I'd trust the pair of them with my life. In fact, I am trusting them with my life, and Vanni too, working the shovel beside me as we dig. I don't think the dentist is going to be disappointed with the workmanship of his new driveway which—when we've finished, sometime in the early hours of tomorrow morning—will be as smooth and black as the surface of an ebony lake, as an onyx horizon. Like a familial bond, it'll be solid and it'll go down deep, deeper than it strictly needs to. It will last that man—should he take care of it—a lifetime, and more besides.

◇◇◇◇◇◇

Working Overtime

Matt Phillips

◇◇◇◇◇◇

Know thyself.

That's how Mantra's daddy used to put it.

Know thyself, motherfucker.

His daddy, all seven feet two of him, humping ass down the baby food aisle at Kmart, looking for blueberry-banana puree to mix with his 25oz of Rolling Rock. Mantra couldn't help thinking about the man, wondering what in the fuck happened to him. What he said in his head was, you can wonder all you want—it ain't going to give you no answers, motherfucker. Then he thought about the phrase, no answers. No, he told himself, say it like this: Know answers.

Know answers, motherfucker.

That's as far as he went with it because he got a hunger for nicotine and lit a cigarette, sat smoking in the driver's seat of a broke-ass Jeep Cherokee he lifted at the outlet mall near Beaumont. One-eighty-thou on the motherfucker; the in-line six growled like a Slurpee machine the whole way back to Palm Springs. So bad that Mantra said fuck it. Started blasting Top 40 hits out of a local radio station, power one hundred and something.

He leaned back in the seat and squinted at the bungalow.

It was dark already—six in the evening—and there was one light on in the living room. Every now and then, Mantra caught a shadow passing through

TOUGH

or partly blocking out the light. Sheila, maybe. Or the Dude.

That fucking piece-of-shit Dude.

Little downtown Palm Springs bungalow. This fucking dude. Mantra couldn't believe Sheila fucked the man. He puffed out smoke and watched the street. Wide lanes with those rounded curbs, palm trees and eucalyptus swaying high above them. The Jeep's driver's side window was lowered slightly and Mantra could smell the flowering oleanders and a hedge of roses in the bungalow's front yard.

All right, Dude. Nice place you got.

Little Palm Springs joint, huh?

A fuck pad, huh?

Mantra finished the cigarette, flicked it out the window. He lit another and kept watching. A shadow appeared in the window, shrank back into the bungalow's mysterious throat. You like that bungalow dick, Sheila. Man, Mantra thought, I never figured you for bungalow dick. Never figured you for wanting to fuck a dude who took tennis lessons and played polo.

Never would have figured.

He was halfway through his second cigarette, watching for more shadows in the bungalow, when his cell phone rang. He picked it up without looking at the caller ID, blew smoke into the mouthpiece. "This is Mantra. What up?"

"Yo, Detective Mantra. This is Louie over in—"

"Louie Ants, that you?"

"Shit, yeah. Course it is, buddy."

"I thought you had a retirement coming up?"

"I do," Louie said. "Shit. I did. I'm doing some part time consulting for the County Sheriff's Department."

"No shit," Mantra said. And then he thought: Know shit.

Know shit, motherfucker.

"Reason I'm calling: We got a body out in the hills. A gangbanger."

"Another one bites the dust, huh?" Mantra watched as the bungalow's light dimmed and a smaller light emerged in the window. Goddamn candle. Now they were lighting candles. "I known a few gangbangers in my time. Let's have it."

Louie gave Mantra the rundown: About five-seven, one-forty. Two tear drops tattooed under the left eye. A bulldog on the right shoulder. Your run-of-the-mill Mother Theresa shit across the abdomen. Some Jesus tats, too.

Mantra asked what kind of shoes. Why's that matter? It just does, Louie. Nike. Okay, what kind of Nike? What do I mean, what kind? Oh, the crime scene techs say Air Force Ones. Is that important? Maybe. Yeah, maybe.

Louie said, "I'm just trying to get an ID on the motherfucker. You know how it is when they don't got a wallet or an RIP tat, right?"

"I know how it is," Mantra said. He watched the candle flicker in the window. How motherfucking romantic. This fucking Dude and Sheila.

"Any of this tug on your balls?"

Mantra said, "You got an eye color for me? What about hair style? They wear the same hair style, usually. Even when they get older."

Louie cleared his throat. "Thing is, he got the top of his head shot off. Only thing I can make out clear is the two tear drops."

"Well," Mantra said, "it must have hurt if he was crying."

That got a laugh and Louie said, "Yeah. It hurt so bad he died."

Mantra didn't laugh. He watched the candle flicker. "None of this is giving me a picture," he said.

"I can't say I ever had the pleasure of meeting your dead man. Not that I can remember, at least."

"You don't know him, huh?"

"Nope. I don't know him."

They hung up and Mantra watched the window and the candle flickering inside it. Too bad, he thought. I didn't know the man. And I couldn't help the man. He flicked his cigarette out the window. Know thyself, he thought.

Know thyself, motherfucker.

◇◇◇◇◇◇

Two days earlier Mantra met Sheila at a donut shop on Slauson, sat chewing a jelly donut while she poured powdered creamer into her Starbucks cup. They sat at a wobbly table and Mantra said, "Not even gonna buy a Bear Claw, huh? You come in here with your upper- middle-class coffee and use the man's creamer. Can't see it in your heart to kick some dough his way?"

Sheila sighed and looked sideways at the glass display with all the rows of donuts and pastries. "This fucker has enough dough, if you ask me."

No fighting Sheila, Mantra decided.

He slurped red jam through his lips and asked her why the fuck she was taking him away from his perfect LA day chatting up suspected murderers and letting widows cry on his cold shoulder.

"Because I can, that's why," she said. "You're my brother-in-law, right?"

"Only by marriage." Mantra smiled, dabbed at his front teeth with a big purple tongue. "You know, I got a real job, Sheila. I can't be taking time to eat donuts and talk about getting our nails done."

"Like Randle doesn't have a real job?"

"My brother—older brother, mind you—teaches second grade."

"Exactly."

"The man sits around doing basic arithmetic and taking attendance."

Sheila sipped her coffee and shook her head. "You're such a prick, Mantra. Just because you're a cop, you think you're so fucking important."

"I got a gun and a badge."

"And a pencil-slim dick to match."

Mantra exhaled through his nose, got serious. It wasn't like Sheila to talk that way, especially not with her husband's little brother. He wiped his sticky fingers with a napkin. "What's wrong, Sheila?"

"Nothing."

"Sheila, what's wrong?"

"I called you because..."

It sat there on her face. In her eyes. Something deep and unspoken and too dangerous to put into the hot air of a Slauson Avenue donut shop. Mantra saw a few lies cross her mind, saw them emerge in the wrinkles at her mostly smooth temples, in the sharp points that formed the outside of her eyes, in the slightest twinge of an upper lip. You get so good—as a cop—that you can see a lie before it crosses a person's lips. But Sheila didn't lie. Mantra had to give her that. She didn't lie to him. Instead, she trailed off and sat there scratching the top of one hand with a manicured fingernail—a blood-red fingernail. Mantra put a hand on top of hers and said, "If something's wrong, Sheila—if something's wrong, I'm here to help. We're family."

"Yeah. I mean, no—nothing's wrong. I just..."

"What?"

"I have to go. I-I forgot about something. I'm sorry, Mantra. Thanks for meeting me, okay? I just...I have to go." And she did.

He watched her through the donut shop's window as she hustled across the parking lot, climbed into her leased BMW. Black as night and sleek as an insect. She pulled onto Slauson and headed east.

Something's wrong all right, Mantra thought. Wrong as fuck.

He started tailing her that evening.

◇◇◇◇◇◇

And now, here ye sit, he thought. Watching your brother's wife suck off some country club Dude with a Maserati and a Palm Springs bungalow. Mantra started the Jeep and cruised past the bungalow, squinted at the flickering candle in the front window. He didn't know what to do. His brother was at a teacher's retreat in Ojai. Should he call and let Randle know his wife was fucking somebody else? Or just drive back to LA and let it ride? Was this any business of his? Mantra turned the Jeep onto Palm Canyon, the town's main drag, and headed south through trinket shops and quaint Italian restaurants. After a few blocks, he parked on the street. He locked the Jeep and walked into a Tiki Bar—the sweat rolling off his face dried with the cool air conditioning inside the place.

The decor was pure Polynesian, warrior masks and palm fronds. The bar was already full this early in the evening; Mantra found a spot on the patio overlooking the street. It was hot on the patio—despite the hoses spraying cool mist—and he ordered a piña colada. The drink arrived and Mantra sipped it while he thought about his brother.

His only brother.

Yeah, they were close. Did everything together as kids. Mantra played quarterback in high school and he set a few records throwing to Randle, the all-city receiver. They went off to separate colleges—Mantra at LA City and Randle in the Midwest.

Randle became a teacher.

Mantra became a cop.

Know thyself, motherfucker.

Sheila and Randle got married fast. Too fast for Mantra's comfort. But he saw the man happy—really happy, that is—for the first time since their dad got put away. Sent upstate to the joint. All seven feet two inches of him.

And Randle and Mantra never saw the man again.

Last Mantra checked, their dad was a ghost.

Let out of prison in 2010 and nowhere to be found.

For what? For killing their momma. Well, for getting her killed.

Drunk driving down—wouldn't you know it?—Slauson Avenue on a Thursday night. You can bet the phrase is real: Cars do wrap themselves around telephone poles. Or people wrap cars around telephone poles.

And that was the heart of it—Sheila looked like momma. Talked like her. Hell, sometimes you looked at Sheila and thought: That must be momma's reincarnation. But it wasn't weird that Randle fell in love with Sheila.

She was different, too.

Had a little hustle in her.

Some kind of hot fire.

And it looked like she was burning Randle. No-goddamn-way. No way in hell. No-goddam-way. Nobody burns my brother. I'm a LA city homicide cop

and nobody—no-fucking-body—burns my brother.
Mantra took the final sip of his piña colada.

He had a bungalow to visit.

◇◇◇◇◇◇

Another cigarette.

Mantra puffed and watched. The candle in the bungalow's window was out, but another light was on deep inside the place. In another window. The bedroom, probably. He puffed and puffed. Sat there seething and thinking and breathing. At about nine that night, he got another call.

"This Mantra. What up?"

"Mantra? It's me."

"Randle?"

"Yeah, man."

"I thought you were up in Ojai?"

"I am," Randle said. "Got about three more inclusivity modules to attend."

"Watch you ma-call-it?"

Randle chuckled and said, "Man, if anybody needs sensitivity training, it's you. I bet you drive around looking for people to shoot."

"Somebody's got to do it."

"Right," Randle said. "Hey, bro: You mind driving over to my place and checking on Sheila? She was supposed to go out for dinner with a friend, but she should be back by now. I can't get ahold of her."

Mantra stared bullets at the lighted window.

"It's just, you know, I want to make sure she's okay."

"Yeah, I know."

"What?"

"You want to make sure she's okay," Mantra said. But he thought: She sure as shit ain't okay. And you won't be either, Randle.

"You can try to call, but she's not answering."

"I hear you," Mantra said. "I'll head over there now. I'm sure she's fine."

"Yeah, me too." Randle clicked his teeth. "It's just, you know..."

"Yeah, I know. Let me call you back."

"Cool. Thanks, bro."

Mantra pushed the end call button. As he did, the bungalow's living room light flashed on. He saw two shadows cross through the light and then it went out again. The bungalow's front door opened and two silhouettes moved into view on the stone walkway. Mantra watched Sheila and the Dude move down the driveway past the gleaming Maserati and stand waiting on the curb. The Dude looked Mantra's way, punched a button on his phone. Sheila stood there in a white gown; the gown clung to her figure like stretch fabric. God, he thought, she does look a bit like momma. What Mantra wondered:

What are they doing?

And then he saw headlights flash in the Jeep's rearview mirror.

Ride share. Here Sheila was with her Palm Springs Dude and they were going out for a night on the town. Maybe get a little drunk and cruise back to the bungalow, have a nice Palm Springs fuck. And with Randle pulling his pud up in Ojai.

God, Mantra thought. Damn.

He acted without thinking—he felt a surge of anger run through him and he twisted the Jeep's ignition key, slammed his foot against the gas pedal. The vehicle shot forward, crossed through the gaze of headlights behind him. He saw the Dude's face squirm into a frown and—for an instant—he saw Sheila's eyes glaze in fear. He ran them down and knew they were both dead. Their bodies made thumping sounds—thump-thump-thump like a boxer hitting a bag—against the bumper and along the undercarriage. He stopped the Jeep and the tires squealed. The car behind him stopped too and Mantra sat there bathed in the headlights and his own uncontrollable rage. Nobody but nobody fucks with my brother, he told himself.

Nobody but no-fucking-body.

He slammed the throttle again and steered the Jeep onto the main drag. He sped toward the freeway and, when he was headed west on Interstate 10 toward Los Angeles, he picked up his phone and called his brother.

"She okay?" Randle asked. He had a wheeze in his voice. Like he'd been running. Or like he'd been worried as hell. "You find out if she's okay?"

"Yeah," Mantra said. "She's all right. Trust me, brother. She's just fine."

◇◇◇◇◇

And They Shall Take Up Serpents

Chris McGinley

◇◇◇◇◇◇

There were no pews to speak of in the Coombs County Holiness Church. But in and amongst the folding chairs were some newly made pine benches that counteracted the moldy smell of the old cinder block building. Harlan and James sat together on one of them and watched the preacher testify. He held a pair of timber rattlers in each hand and boomed out scripture and admonishment. His hair was matted with sweat and his tie loosened. One of his shirttails had come untucked. Here and there, congregants convulsed and shouted proclamations. A few held snakes and howled streams of gibberish.

The boys had seen it all before.

"Preacher's puttin' on a good show today," Harlan said, just loud enough for James to hear.

James laughed through his nose. "You're too cynical, man. What's it to you if he believes in something besides oxycontin?"

Harlan smiled and revealed a dull silver cuspid. "Oh, you're a funny one, you are. You should consider a career in comedy."

"Someday," James covered his smile with his hand. "Stop now. We gotta do this thing."

When it was over the congregants lit cigarettes and piled into cars. A few stragglers and zealots hung around and talked with one another. A married couple hopped on an ATV and tore out onto the road, the fat wheels of the vehicle throwing gravel everywhere. With their Mountain Dews in hand, the boys waited by the church van to talk to the preacher.

"Now how's your momma, James?" The preacher lit a cigarette and blew the smoke up in the air.

"She's ok, Reverend. She's got the cancer, you know. But she said to tell you she's gonna make it back to church one of these days."

"You tell her I'm prayin' for her. And what about your daddy, Harlan? Has he been to that clinic like I told him?"

"Yessir, he has. They got him an oxygen tank and some medicine to help him breathe. Thank you, Reverend."

"By God," the preacher said, "Black lung. Coal keeps us and kills us, don't it?"

"Yessir," the boys answered.

"So, you wanna borrow the van, right?" the preacher asked, his cigarette bobbing up and down as he reached into his pocket for the keys.

"Yessir," James said. "We got all kinds of baseball equipment to move out of the gym and into the building by the field."

"Can't you use your pickup?"

"No, sir," Harlan answered. "We need something enclosed, something with lots of room. Otherwise we'll have to make four or five trips."

The preacher gave Harlan the keys and told the boys to be careful. Get the van back by tomorrow night, he said, and avoid the devil's temptations, by God.

They agreed to all the terms and James followed Harlan to his trailer in the pickup.

◇◇◇◇◇◇

"Look at this goddamn piece of shit," Harlan said in the driveway.

James gave the van a once over, though he had seen it hundreds of times before in the church lot. The once white Econoline was hand painted in a wild mix of upper and lower case letters, covered in scripture and misspellings. They shall take up serpints. And if they drink any dedly thing, it shall not hurt them. They shall lay hands on the sick, and they shall recuver.

"Could've used a proofreader," James said.

Harlan shook his head. "Look at the state of it. Has he ever thought to clean it out? What would the Lord think of this kind of tribute?" He pulled on a half pint of Early Times and handed it over to James. "Fuckin' fast food bags and cups all over the dashboard. By God!"

James laughed and pointed a finger at Harlan. "Mocking a man of the Lord. That's sinful, you." He pulled on the bottle and looked in the windows of the van. "Well, so long as it gets up up that mountain and back down, I don't care what state it's in. The whole point is cover. Cops ain't gonna stop a church van."

"Yeah, let's hope so. And we'll need to move the baseball stuff afterward. To make it look good. Make sure Coach knows we're doing it, too."

"That part's easy," James said. "I just want to get up on that hill, get the shit, get it to Jubal's, and get paid."

"Damn straight," Harlan said.

Inside the trailer, Harlan's father sat on a La-Z-Boy and watched a game show. A tv tray of remote controls, a spit cup, and a vial of prescription pills sat within reach. There was a stack of official-looking letters from doctors and the insurance company, all demanding money or referencing some previous dispute. There were explanations of denials for coverage and urgent declarations of past due dates and actions to follow. Harlan had been reading them for years. Once he even wondered if the same person had written all of them. Each one sounded exactly like the next. The old man's oxygen tank sat on the floor on a little hand truck with wheels, though the only traffic it ever got was to and from the bathroom, bedroom, and kitchen. He said something to the boys that got lost in the oxygen mask and they nodded. Thirty years in a deep mine and fighting the insurance company for the last fifteen to see if he could buy another ten. That was his story. There were a lot like it around there.

"You need anything, Dad?" Harlan asked.

He lifted the mask long enough to say, "I need you to stay away from drugs is what I need."

Harlan rolled his eyes and slumped down on the couch with James. They passed the bottle back and forth. Then it was Harlan's dad who rolled his eyes.

"It ain't drugs, Dad. Just a little snort now and again. Good for a man," Harlan said.

Lifting the mask, his father hissed, "You got to live righteous."

"Yup, tryin' to. We just got back from church, matter of fact."

Harlan's father nodded an approval and the three of them sat there, the game show blaring, until Harlan judged enough time spent to justify a departure. "We're gonna go out, Dad. You need anything?"

Harlan's father shook his head and extended his hand in a gesture that nearly made James cry every time he witnessed it. Harlan rose and took the old man's bony hand. He held it in both his own and rubbed it gently, his fingers going over the collapsed veins that ran under the paper thin skin full of liver spots. Finally, he kissed the old man's hand and placed one of his own on the back of his father's neck, giving it a little squeeze.

It was the same thing his father used to do when Harlan was just a little boy.

◇◇◇◇◇◇

At around 4:00 a.m., there was no one else on the mining road. Still, Harlan drove carefully, and though the boys passed a pint of whiskey back and forth, they took only tiny sips. "A little for courage," James said. Harlan slowed to navigate a hairpin on the steep slope.

"What are you gonna do with your share?" Harlan asked.

"Don't know. My mom's behind on rent, again. So help out, I guess."

"Where you gonna say you got the money, dumbass?" The van slowed as it climbed the narrow mountain road, and something in the back slid and banged against the rear doors. "What was that?" Harlan said.

James turned to look but he couldn't see anything. "Not sure. Nothing important. Drive on, Jeeves." He looked in the back again, but didn't see anything. Then he said, "Where do I say I got the money? She knows better than to ask that these days. What you gonna do with yours?"

"Two words, my friend. Oxy Contins."

The boys laughed and James said, "Was it you who done the lettering job on this van?"

Harlan chuckled, "I will try to pay some of them medical bills. But it's a losing battle, you know? Fuckin' coal company. The guy worked, like, 30 some years, and the insurance is refusing to pay for half the stuff he needs."

"The system's fucked. All of Appalachia is fucked, actually. I can't wait to get outta here someday."

"Yup. Someday. That's what they all say."

"Tell you what," James said. "The day my dad died, I declared war on the company. On all coal companies, I mean. That's why I don't mind stealing from them. I'll use the money I steal to get the hell out of Kentucky once and for all. It's justified theft, way I see it. You oughta see it that way, too. Your dad is going the same way mine did, not to be morbid. Same stuff, though. Black lung, the respirator, the drugs, the letters from the insurance agency. Same stuff I saw for years. My old man dying was a blessing, in a way. Fuck this place. Fuck coal."

In the preacher's voice Harlan said, "Coal keeps us and kills us." He took a sip of the whiskey and passed it over to James. The van leveled out on a stretch near the top of the mountain and picked up a little speed. "So, I'm justified in stealing this shit because of my dad's situation, you're saying?"

"Damn straight," James answered. He took a sip of the whiskey.

"Good to know. You think the judge will go for that if we get arrested?"

James laughed in spite of himself, "Don't even joke about something like that."

Harlan slowed down as they neared the outbuildings furthest from the strip site. "Seriously, though. I'm with you. If I could leave today I would. But I can't. Not just because of my dad."

"Why, then?" James asked.

Harlan capped the whiskey bottle and slowed the van to a crawl, craning his neck and scoping the area. "Well, I don't know where I'd go or what I'd do. I mean, when we finish school. If we finish, that is, what are we gonna do with high school degrees? I don't know anyone outside of these hills. Do you? And you know something else? Everybody we know who left this place has come back. Every godddamn one. Hill folks are like fish out of water anywhere else. It's crazy, but I don't think I could make it outside these hills."

"You're not making it now, Coal Miner's Daughter. We gotta steal to pay our parents' rent and medical bills. This is one fucked-up cycle we're in. We need to get out, boy."

"Yeah, maybe. Look, let's get this done. We'll talk about it later." Harlan scoped the area again and pulled the van close to one of the outbuildings. "That's the one Jubal said's got the tools and the saws. We grab those, rip out the wiring, and we're outta here. Let's go." He opened his door.

"Hold up," James said.

"What?"

"Let's just listen for a minute. We haven't done anything yet. We ain't in trouble. So just listen. See if you hear anything first."

"What the fuck are you talking about, man? There's nobody up here."

James took a deep breath and let it out through his nose. "You know, there's supposed to be a haint up here."

Harlan laughed. "Jethro, there ain't no such thing. Jesus, you do need to get out of these hills."

"I'm just sayin', let's be careful. There's been some accidents up here. Jubal said one of the guys he used to work with saw a haint one night, just as the sun went down, and the dude got his neck broke out here the very next day. He said she attacks the workers because of what they're doing to the mountain. She comes outta the woods. That's the story, anyway. That's what Jubal said. Lots of guys getting hurt on this site."

"Hellfire, a tree-hugger haint. Wonder what the preacher would think of that? It's a woman? Is she, like, a hippie? Good-looking, did the guy say? Before he broke his neck, I mean?"

"Fuck you. Let's go." James unscrewed the bottle and took a long pull. The boys opened the back doors of the van.

"Shit! This is what we heard before," James said, pushing aside a low wood box. "A fuckin' snake box." He moved closer to get a good look. "And there's snakes in it. Goddamn preacher. Leaves them in the van."

"I didn't see anything back here before," Harlan said.

"Must've been under the bench," James answered. At the disturbance, one of the snakes sounded its rattle, a long hiss that rose and fell, then rose and fell again.

"By God," Harlan said. "It's Satan's work we're doin'. The snake's trying to tempt us."

The boys laughed as James sat a heavy tire iron on top of the box. Their gear in hand now and head-lamps on, they moved away. Jubal had a key made of the outbuilding and the boys were in quickly. They found the tools in a storage room and made several trips to the van. Once Harlan hauled out the copper wire, they broke a window on Jubal's instructions and headed to the van. It was a done deal.

But Harlan thought he heard something when he tossed the wire and his tools in the the back of the van. "What the fuck was that?" He flipped on his head lamp and the two of them looked toward the trees just beyond the access road into the site. A shock of long white hair flew out from behind the large trunk of an elm and disappeared again.

"Shit! Did you see that?"

"I sure as hell did," said James. "Let's get outta here. C'mon, hurry up with that shit."

As Harlan tossed in the bag of tools the hiss of a rattler startled him. "Shut up, you." When he moved to close the van doors, the the snake got him on the hand. "Goddamn!" he yelled.

"Fuck," James said. A lone rattler slithered down onto the pavement and headed in the direction of the tree line. The other snakes in the box began to hiss all at once. "Goddamn. Did he get you deep?" James asked. "He must've got out when the box slid against the door. Shit. Is it a deep bite? Is it a dry bite, or wet?"

"Hell if I know," Harlan said. "Motherfucker!" Fear was rising in him and he started to sweat.

"I'll drive," James said. "We gotta get you to the clinic. They got anti-venom there, don't worry, brutha. I saw a med kit in the building. Let me get that first. Gotta put a bandage on it. Let it bleed for a few minutes, though. Be right back. You're gonna be ok, man. You gotta breathe slowly. Take deep breaths. Don't accelerate your heart rate."

James ran toward the outbuilding, got inside with Jubal's key, ripped the med kit from the wall, and headed back to the van. Harlan was gone. James looked around and called for him, but got no answer. He felt the sweat falling in beads from his temples and he could hear his own heartbeat in his ears.

Then there was a muffled sound that came from the woods across the access road. James flipped on his headlamp and rushed over. When he got close he thought he saw some movement deeper into the woods where he heard something rustling in the brush. There was another sound, too, like a bobcat's wail, but lower, more guttural. He thought he saw a flash of white moving deep in there.

For an hour he looked for Harlan, first walking in the woods, and then driving the van all over the site and calling out his name. But when he saw the first signs of light in the sky, he knew he had to go. He told himself over and over that no one dies from a snakebite, and that surely Harlan would have enough sense to say nothing about the robbery when they found him.

Eventually, he made it to Jubal's and unloaded the gear. He didn't bother with details, though, just said that Harlan had to get home to his daddy. He took Harlan's cut for him and Jubal knew enough about the friends that he didn't suspect anything shady. The next day, James moved the baseball equipment with the assistant coach and returned the van. It was only later, when Harlan didn't turn up, that Jubal began to wonder about James' story. But what could he do, except wonder? He sure as hell couldn't go to the cops and explain that the boys were up on the strip site and that they should search for Harlan there.

Strange as it was, though, it wasn't the cops that Jubal was most worried about. "That goddamn haint," he said to himself. "Damn that goddamn haint."

At some point, Harlan finally fell down at a spot deep in the woods. And that's where it happened. There was definite pain, a hard throbbing in his hand and arm. But there was something else, too, a feeling not exactly like the oxy he loved so much, but more like that acid he took that time with James. He lay on his back in the leaves and looked up through the tree canopy. The light was coming in pale patches and he thought he felt the sun on his skin. But now his breathing seemed to come easier and he began to feel a heightened sense of things. There was the raw smell of the wet earth, and now and again the sound of a red-tailed hawk somewhere nearby. Harlan let himself take it all in. He was no longer worried, even when the timber rattler sounded somewhere close to him. Then, just before he went out, he was sure he saw her. She stood above him, naked and covered in splotches of dried black earth, her wrinkled breasts hanging flat against her torso and her skin sagging at the joints. The knees were rubbed raw and trails of blood, dried to almost black now, ran down the shins and over the feet. The last thing he remembered was the snake. It had begun to slither up her leg, but she took no notice. The sound it made now was deafening.

◇◇◇◇◇◇

Harlan's body was never found and James never got out. Years later he was still working at the welding and metal fabricators' shop where he got on after high school. But it seemed like they were always cutting into his hours. Once in awhile he would run into a miner who knew someone who supposedly saw the boy haint. It was always second and third-hand stuff, though. Inevitably, the story ended with an injury to someone on the mining site where the boy was seen. Some people thought the sites were cursed, and, supposedly anyway, some miners wouldn't even work them, though James never met any such person. He always listened to the stories, politely, expressing wonderment at all the appropriate places. But he tried not to give the story much mind.

Still, he had a tough time of it when someone would mention the haint's scar, one that ran from fingers to elbow. The telltale sign of a snakebite.

run, Jennifer

doungjai gam

◇◇◇◇◇

Friday evening at Shenanigans and happy hour is in full swing. Rob sighs when he sees the party of ten come roaring through the door, ablaze in their loud polo shirts and even louder blather.

Elizabeth comes over and drops her happy hostess façade. "I'm sorry," she mutters. "Yours is the only ten top open."

"It's fine. The way my day's been going, how much worse can it get?"

"You really want me to answer that?" Their laughter reeks of bitterness.

After tending to his other customers, Rob grits his teeth and takes a deep breath before approaching the table. "Hey guys, welcome back to Shenanigans! I'm Rob and I'll be taking care of you tonight and—hey, Jennifer! Good to see ya."

"Hi Rob!" She gets up to hug him. She's the only one not wearing a company polo and she looks out of place in her dress slacks, blouse and pink highlighted hair.

"What are you doing hanging with these guys?" He points to her coworkers, hoping that his smile looks natural.

"I just started working with them a couple of weeks ago."

"Very nice."

"Rob is a friend of my brother Errick," she tells the group, who smile in utter fake interest while he takes their drink orders.

He hates judging people, but he's waited on this group before and they've never struck him to be anything more than empty suits who give out unwanted nicknames and crappy tips. Their polo shirts range from pale to bright red, all bearing their corporate logo.

Whether it's on the streets or in a cubicle seat, gang colors all the same.

As the evening rolls on, customers come and go but the raucous corporate party sticks around, drinking and occasionally snacking on a half-price appetizer. He brings Jennifer another beer and tries not to glare at the guy next to her, a blond dudebro whose hands like to roam. Rob's seen him in here many times with his coworkers and on dates, never with the same woman twice. Kevin, he's sure his name is. Rob sees Kevin's hand on Jennifer's knee, inching up ever so slowly. She looks uncomfortable but none of her coworkers seem to notice or care.

She excuses herself and damn near runs to the bathroom, purse in hand. Rob overhears her coworkers talking as he reads the specials to the table next to them.

"What is with the pink hair?"

"She's an odd one. Did you see what she was eating for lunch the other day?"

Then the dudebro chimes in, his voice grating: "Don't be talking about my girl Jenny like that."

His declaration is met with "Dude, you wish!" and much laughter. He responds with, "You just wait, you just wait" on a loop as if repetition will make it true. He hears them call out to him, "Hey Roberto, we're thirsty!" and ignores them.

On his way back to the kitchen Rob runs into Jennifer.

"Hey." She smiles. Her face is pale and one hand clutches at her stomach.

"You okay?"

She shakes her head. "I feel...off. Anxiety's kicking in hard."

"Nice bunch of coworkers you have."

"They're not my type, especially..." She trails off, leaving Kevin's name unspoken.

"If you don't feel good, you should go home. Fuck 'em."

After a moment's thought, she reaches into her purse and gives him a fifty. "Can I pay my portion now? I'm going to go back and tell them I'm not feeling well."

"Sure thing." He cashes her out and writes two words on her twenty. When he brings her change over he hands it to her so that the message is visible. She looks at it and nods, handing him a healthy tip.

"It was so great to see you, Rob. I'll see you soon." She hugs him and whispers, "Thank you."

Kevin stands up too quickly and wobbles. "I'll walk you to your car."

"I'm fine, thanks." She gives Rob's hand a quick squeeze before dashing away.

While the corporate schlubs razz on Kevin's failure, Rob heads to the bathroom. It's another hour until his shift is up but he can't wait that long. Happy hour is long over and the bar is quieter now. While he washes his hands, someone bangs on the door. "Be right out," he says.

The second he unlocks the door it flies open and whacks him in the face. Stunned, he staggers back and sees Kevin's ugly sneering face looming in on him fast.

"Motherfucker," Kevin says as he locks the door.

"The hell, man?" Rob tries to maintain his friendly waiter face but that mask is melting fast.

"I saw what you wrote on her change. Who you want her to run from?" Kevin's in his face now, all loaded up on alcoholic swagger.

"You need to get out of my way. And once you're done pissing, don't even bother washing your hands. I want you to get the fuck out of here."

Kevin growls as he charges and knocks Rob back against the wall. Rob shakes his head and notices the other feeling around in his pockets for something. He takes advantage of this and grabs him by his overstyled hair and bashes the side of his head against the sink. The wannabe ladies' man slumps and falls to the floor. Rob pats the guy down and finds a switchblade and a vial of clear liquid in his pants pocket.

That piece of shit. He wonders how many of the ladies he'd come in with had fallen for his average looks and slobbering attempts to slide right in, and how many of them became another unwilling unknowing bedpost notch.

It takes all of Rob's might to not open the switchblade and finish the job. Instead, he grabs the bottle and dumps the contents straight down Kevin's wretched gullet. He immediately gags and coughs as he struggles to get up off the floor. He grabs him by the hair again and slams his head into the sink – once, twice, and one more time for good measure. Finally the sonuvabitch goes quiet.

Rob pokes his head out of the bathroom and sees no one around. Working as fast as he can, he grabs Kevin underneath his arms and lifts him. He drags the guy down the hall past the kitchen to the back door. Once outside, he bangs his head one last time against the side of the dumpster and shoves him in through the door. He considers closing it, but if it's open it could look more like an accident, that in his inebriated state he could have been looking for a place to get steady and then—whoops.

He wouldn't be the first drunk that ended up in their dumpster.

Rob heads in, making a stop at the bathroom to fix his hair and make sure the scene is clean. He curses when he spots a cell phone under the sink— how did I miss that before? The lock screen photo is a terrible selfie of the scumbag with a girl who is all teeth and mascara. He powers the phone down and rushes back outside. All is quiet in the dumpster. He wipes it down before tossing it in the trash and walking back in.

One last bathroom check and now all is good. He starts for his section only to be stopped by Elizabeth.

"Your ten top is demanding their check."

Rob readies their check and puts on his best smile as he hurries over, where they're sloshed and laughing about who knows what.

"Hey, have you seen our friend? This guy here." One of them motions at the empty chair next to him. "He went to the bathroom and he hasn't come back yet."

He pretends to think. "I'm pretty sure I saw him heading out the back door. He looked like he needed some fresh air."

They laugh at this and talk over each other:

"Fucking Kevin."

"He's probably trying to skip out on the bill."

"I'll cover his beers...he owes me for this."

They pay their check and predictably leave a terrible tip. Rob watches them from the bar as they leave. A couple of guys go around back. Rob waits for something—a scream, any of them to come rushing back in demanding justice, a blast of sirens.

But nothing comes.

◇◇◇◇◇◇

Love-Honor-Cherish

J.D. Graves

◇◇◇◇◇◇

"You know my wife," Tom told the grocer, "and you know what they say, happy wife equals happy life."

The grocer smiled and nodded despite the fact no one had seen Carmen Sloane for five years. Her husband, Tom, on the other hand was always around. Tom stopped by weekly and purchased the same thing every time: box of Fels-Naptha, four large pork roasts, and a gallon of apple sauce. The grocer rang up the total, watching with a pained patient smile as his best customer counted out spare change. Tom ignored the exasperated sighs of the people queuing behind him. A few patrons put their meager items back or dropping them where they stood before bolting for another bodega.

The grocer spoke up, "Tom, I--"

"Yeah?" Tom asked without ceasing his count.

"I just wanted to let you know that, there was a detective come in yesterday asking about you."

"Asking about me?"

"About you--your wife mainly. I told him you were one of my best customers, like clockwork. He wanted to know what items you bought."

"Did you tell him?" Tom asked finishing his math.

"No, I told him to beg off."

"You shouldn't do that, not to a policeman, they have a tough job. They deserve our respect. Listen

if you see him again tell him where I live, I'd be happy
to answer any questions he might have."

"You sure you wanna do that?" The grocer said
sweeping the coins into his tray without recounting
them.

"Absolutely, me and Carmen got nothing to hide."

Tom gathered his purchases and left. He
pretended the news of the detective didn't bother
him. He ignored the whispers behind his back as he
walked down the street. Suspicious words about
the man whom everyone believed murdered his wife.
Tom knew Carmen was very much alive. He knew too
that no one, in her present condition, could ever see
her to verify that fact.

It was impossible.

The damage to his reputation and her good name
would be catastrophic. So he allowed the hushed
accusations to continue unabated. He donned an
air of unflappable good humor and took the time to
chat up acquaintances anytime they passed. Always
assuring them of Carmen's good health. All part of
his daily regimen. Tom knew the truth. And since Dr.
Fielding's accident Tom was the only one left alive
who knew. Although Carmen lived, her quality of life
remained questionable.

Tom knew, it wasn't always this way. In the
beginning, like all beginnings, Carmen's beauty
turned heads everywhere she went. Tom sometimes wondered, how he got so lucky to have met
her, wed her and bed her. But he did. He fell into
the euphoria of love. The euphoria never stays long
once the honeymoon is over and both spouses reveal
their warts and farts. How does one maintain a
marriage, without it falling into humdrum boredom
or completely apart?

At stressful times, Tom remembered the vows he spoke that warm day in June so many years ago. Anytime he felt overwhelmed, Tom remembered his promise, in sickness and in health. It pacified most notions of fleeing.

Tom felt certain other men would've fled at the first sign of trouble. If the shoe were on the other foot, he prayed Carmen, with her charming good looks, would've kept her vows too. Personal sacrifice, he reasoned, is a learned trait.

Every day he walked the twelve blocks to work and home. He didn't mind the trek, it established a mind-clearing routine and provided good exercise. He'd return home later to care for his wife and agonize over the mountain of medical bills. He could file for bankruptcy, but he knew he'd lose not only his wife but his small business as well. SLOANE'S SNACKS was the only mom and pop vending machine company left in Queens.

Before he met Carmen, his business was his pride and joy. These days however, just a means to an end. At its height, SLOANE'S SNACKS profited two million a year with a fleet of seven trucks and twenty employees. When the law passed making junk food and soda almost forbidden, all of Tom's business slimmed. He still owned the warehouse and their apartment building, but they were the only tenants and he was the only one loading the truck, driving the route and collecting coins. The number of machines dropped just enough to keep the lights on in Carmen's room.

She grew agitated and thrashed about anytime it went dark. Tom empathized. He'd be disgruntled too, if he'd been plunged into a black solitude with little communication, besides muffled grunts. But he loved her all the same and knew the feeling was mutual.

As Tom entered their apartment he could already smell her from downstairs, a moldering fetid aroma. He realized he couldn't remember the last time he'd checked in on her or given her a bath for that matter. How long had it been? Tom feared his days blended together. Surely it hadn't been longer than a week at the most.

Under her room Tom installed a drain pipe that led to the downstairs kitchen sink. This drain became necessary when Tom realized Carmen's mobility was no longer possible. He ducked under it setting aside the soap, apple-sauce and put three of the four pork roasts in the fridge. He knew she'd be hungry but it would have to wait. Her body odor demanded tending. When he passed by her room, the one they'd reserved for a nursery, her stink repelled him.

"Gee whiz honey."

Tom bit his lip in disgust pressing onward for the upstairs bathroom to fill the five buckets with soapy water. He sat on the edge of the tub as water gushed out the spout. It needed to be hot, by the time he carted each bucket to her room the water would've begun to chill. Carmen never responded well to a cold bath, and He wanted to avoid anything extraneous tonight. Besides it was the little touches that reminded her of his commitment.

Tom let the water and his mind run. He remembered after their honeymoon Carmen expressing a desire for a baby. Tom was more than pleased to make his beautiful wife happy and relished every romp.

They tried for months.

Every time, Carmen checked her status she saw the same pink dash, like a sinister hyphen between their vows to each other and the family she wanted. She would go on for days, in distraught fits and rages. At the height of this despair, Tom often worried Carmen might leave him.

Except for lack of pregnancy, Tom considered their marriage comfortable, yet Carmen saw their inability to conceive as monumental.

They visited their physician, initial tests revealed nothing wrong on Tom's part, but Carmen's tests were inconclusive. At their physician's recommendation, the Sloanes submitted to the conventional treatments.

In Vitro Fertilization at the time cost ten thousand dollars a pop. Tom was happy to write the check, besides business boomed. Each IVF treatment, just a drop in the bucket and it pacified Carmen's growing anxieties. A happy wife doesn't guarantee a happy life, but it's a good start. However, after the eleventh failed treatment. Tom wanted to pursue other options.

So began their relationship with Dr. Fielding's Fertility Clinic. Fielding suggested they try his new, unorthodox approach, the Athena Process. Tom's semen would be injected directly into Carmen's ovaries. During her cycle, at least one already fertilized ovum would drop into her uterus, partially formed. The Athena Process sounded like the right medicine for the Sloane's despite its ridiculous price.

Dr. Fielding warned the couple about minor side effects. Tom brushed this off as typical fine print, insisting on trying the Athena. Dr. Fielding stopped speaking and looked at Tom. Tom looked into Carmen's eyes, smiled and signed all waivers. After the two separate six-figure checks cleared, Dr. Fielding performed the twenty-minute procedure.

"Only time will tell," Tom remembered the Doctor saying.

However, the month passed with no changes.

Dr. Fielding suggested they try again. Tom wasted little time writing a second set of checks, even though Carmen seemed less than enthused.

"It's a lot of money, honey," Tom recalled her saying, although he couldn't place his own response. He noticed a growing divide between them. Right around the time SLOANE'S SNACKS began tanking, Carmen spent less time at their apartment. He'd return to a dark home. No food in the kitchen. No wife by his side. She returned later with distance in her voice as she offered plausible excuses: a sick friend, et cetera. However Tom, certain of her duplicity, couldn't help harboring a suspicious heart. One day Tom lied about going to work. He waited around the corner and followed the taxi driving her into the city. To a high rise apartment. To him, her lover.

In the confrontation that followed, Carmen begged and pleaded for Tom to stop. He remembered how she swayed him from killing the other man. How pitiful she looked on her knees groveling and blaming herself. Oh, how she made promises, confessing nothing but love for Tom and only Tom. The gasping whimpers from her lover's bloody body angered Tom, but when he looked into Carmen's crying eyes he couldn't help believing her. He told himself, this is just a bump in the road. What is a successful marriage without them?

Tom forgave her and contacted Dr. Fielding's clinic. The doctor was hesitant, but Tom doubled the check's amount and all parties agreed.

The month passed and finally the glorious day came when Carmen saw a pink plus sign.

She was pregnant.

When the Sloanes made their follow up, Fielding's expression seemed downright shocked. He breathed deep and folded his hands across his desk.

"Please allow me to speak frankly. If I seem surprised it's only because you're the first successful patient who's gone through the Athena."

"How many have you had?" Carmen asked.

"I'm not at liberty to say, as tests are ongoing. But I'm very happy for you. And everything looks normal."

∞∞∞∞∞

Tom felt steam rising off the tub and began filling the buckets, remembering Carmen the night she found the first lump.

It appeared between her breasts near the end of the first trimester. Soft, squeezable and yet firmly rounded as if she'd grown a superfluous third breast. The Sloanes visited their regular physician who ordered a biopsy. The results came back negative for cancer, and the young physician stated that it was a benign tumor filled with healthy cells. He sighed at the couple then added, "I've never seen anything like it before...I don't really know what it is."

Since Carmen was pregnant, surgery would be put off until after delivery. Carmen became despondent over her tripled bust. Tom, try as he might, failed to soothe her. One morning, she awoke to find a new growth on her lower back. A week later, Carmen developed a pair on her abdomen. That morning, the Sloanes stopped by Dr. Fielding's for a sonogram, only to discover their fetus was abnormal. Small and embryonic, far behind schedule for the second trimester. Dr. Fielding sat there perplexed and muttered, "This just can't be."

"What, doctor?" Carmen asked.

Dr. Fielding parsed for the correct explanation, "The fetus has regressed to an even earlier stage of development. It appears to be a zygote again--"

◇◇◇◇◇◇

Tom lined the buckets of water outside Carmen's room. When Tom pressed on the knob, the door didn't budge.

A streak of anxiety rippled across his face. How could she lock the door from inside? Tom leaned in and pushed, hearing the hinges give and squeal. He felt strange pressure from the other side. He pushed again and the door inched open a crack, a sliver of light splashed from the top of the doorway. Tom stepped back realizing to his horror what blocked the door. At once he saw the entire awful picture. He didn't bother asking himself why. He'd known all along that eventually something like this could, nay, would happen.

The night Dr. Fielding died, he called to explain his hypothesis. The Athena had accelerated her fertility and ovulation beyond a quantifiable measurement. Now, Carmen's ovaries, literally contained hundreds of thousands of fertilized eggs that, bombarded her womb every day. This state of constant ovulation, forced her body to reject each old fetus for the new one. But instead of passing them normally, her body absorbed the growing child inside her. Which led Dr. Fielding to conclude, the tumors which emerged at an alarming rate, were in fact fetal manifestations. And worse, she would soon be overtaken. The only way to reverse the condition, required a full hyster-ectomy. This meant they could never have children of their own.

Tom pressed harder against the door and the crack inched open. His fingertips brushed against the flabby flesh that spilled out of Carmen's stinking room.

"She must've fallen over," Tom told himself picturing her body breaking free of the tresses and moorings he'd installed, "Carmen!"

Tom moved a knee into the works heaving into the room, barricaded by Carmen. Her swollen blob-like skin seeped into the hallway. Tom knew he needed to find her face. He needed to check her airway was clear. Tom chucked a hand against her loose billowy body. Tom felt its soft dampness as he clamored his head through the crack and scanned the room.

A sea of naked flesh rippled from wall to wall almost reaching the ceiling.

"Carmen!"

He gripped a fold pulling himself through, crawling delicately across her, sticking his hand in every crease looking for any sign of her hair or her face, but the roomful of sore-covered skin offered no clues.

Carmen was everywhere, and yet she was nowhere to be found.

He traversed this epidermal landscape and slid off to a rare square of floor. On his feet he muscled under her frameless form as this heavy ocean engulfed him.

The smell was worse than ever before, as he crept in the reddish dusk of her body. After much pushing he pressed on, finally finding an eyebrow. He knew the rest of her face was around somewhere. His mind reeled and he remembered, shortly before her body rejected her skeleton and grew out in all directions, the last full words she said that day.

"Please Tom, if we don't find a cure, please don't let me go on like this hideous--"

"You're not hideous," Tom said ignoring the fact that her forehead drooped over her eyes and her cheeks sagged past where her chin once firmly rested.

"I don't want to live like this...if there's no cure."

"Trust me my darling, Dr. Fielding and I won't let that happen."

At that point, Tom was in no condition to tell her the truth. That a patient's husband had rampaged into his clinic, and shot Dr. Fielding full of holes.

Tom could've taken her to see their regular physician for the operation, but he just didn't do it. Besides if she had the operation, she'd never have children, and Tom couldn't bear the thought of her leaving him again.

Now he needn't worry.

Tom could not bring himself, to admit this to her. And on the last day she was able to speak words, he assured her that he loved her and he'd never leave her. For that was the only truth that mattered then as it did now. He knew how lucky she was to have him as her husband, lover and caretaker. Not to mention, father of their children.

Tom navigated his way to her red mouth. The only part of her body that remained attached to her bones. Tom quickly realized she was not breathing. It was too cramped to attempt CPR or any other lifesaving measure.

Carmen was gone.

Tom was too late.

He took her misshapen face and held it close to his own. He was seized with grief. But this grief, quickly dissipated into anger, when Tom realized they weren't alone. Somewhere under the vast corpus of his wife, he heard the tiny muffled coos of another one of those things.

Tom frantically pushed and plodded until he found the source of the noise. And there, bloodied on the floor lay an infant girl still attached to an expelled placenta.

Tom cursed it madly before collecting it and pushing his way out from under Carmen's dead girth into the hallway. He cut the umbilical cord and swaddled it in a dish rag, just like he done for all the others, and made his way to the bathroom.

As he twisted on the cold water, He remembered fondly that first one, so many years ago and how unprepared he was for it. It appeared normal, but Tom knew better. This little pink thing twitching in his hands. Its little toes and fingers fanning out in a state of newborn shock. And then he remembered the noise. The god-awful screams of this tiny creature. And Carmen, his poor dear Carmen, unable to hold the thing or breast feed it, or help Tom in anyway. How she just lay there, propped against the wall in her room. He remembered looking down at the first one with awed disgust, and how much he hated it.

For that small parasitic life form had destroyed his wife.

He remembered how clumsily he disposed of that first one, which Tom recalled distinctly as male. A year would pass before he stopped keeping records of boys and girls. By then he'd fully embraced the proceedings.

The parasites arrived once every two weeks.

Some arrived in pairs.

With Carmen's care his top priority, there was no room in Tom's life for these other things that kept falling out of her. She needed uninterrupted attention, and Tom was more than happy to provide for her, as he'd always done. He was not, however, willing to suffer these horrid creatures any longer than needed. Tom would've preferred to drag out their deaths for he knew, they deserved to suffer, just as they made his wife suffer. But their mere presence aggravated him and he wanted rid of them as soon as possible, so he drowned these horrible things in cold water. The furthest thing from a mother's warm womb.

Tom became very skilled at carrying out the process, and found that it gave him a thrill like no other. He felt like a superhero or Carmen's very own white knight, gallantly arriving and slaying the screaming demons. Once the little things stopped moving, their executioner, would bury their remains in the cellar. Just another set pattern in the routine of his life. No different than brushing one's teeth or picking ticks off the family dog.

Tom placed the stopper in the drain. The lime encrusted spout droned out any audible noise from the bundle of cloth on the tiles.

The water rose and rose. He moved a hand through the water to check the temperature. Satisfied, Tom twisted off the tap. He collected the thing, stood above the tub and submerged his charge in the water. He held her there counting the seconds, one Mississippi, two Mississippi, three...Tom enjoyed watching the life float out of these vermin. He gazed down at the thing under the water and smiled triumphantly at his work.

Tom couldn't help but note certain similarities. The thing looked familiar. He knew in the genetic soup of the womb, each one was different and unique, yet all the same. This pest was particularly cunning, for it had developed certain features of its mother.

A mother it would never know. A woman whose beauty was beyond compare. A woman who had loved Tom, despite everything and vowed to be his wife until death separated them. A sacred vow for a wife whom Tom cared for relentlessly over the years, forgiving all her transgressions. Who, now, was just a moldering lifeless blob.

Tom felt his arms slacken. His wrists relaxed. His fingers still clutched the evil thing, but his mind soared elsewhere. Tom's emotions swelled in him, as he realized that this baby, would be the last one ever. He'd never again feel the joy of being Carmen's champion. Slayer of her demons. Killer of her disease. Keeper of their vows.

Tom pressed forward, if it was going to be the last one, he needed to make it count. He was going to execute it with supreme malice. He stared with dagger eyes at the tiny thing in his hands. But it only smiled back at him from below the water's surface.

Twenty-five Mississippi...

The thing appeared calm.

Twenty-six Mississippi...

It glowed innocence.

Twenty-seven Mississippi...

She radiated love.

Twenty-eight Mississippi...

She looked just like--

Twenty-nine...

Tom looked at the drowning child's face and realized that this need not be the last one ever. He'd need to change his routine, go on an extended hiatus, but in the meantime he'd have someone to care for. Not just anyone, but a newer version of--

He lifted the baby out of the water and patted her intently. The baby appeared to be unharmed by the ordeal. She held no grudge against him and breathed in a calm hiccuping rhythm. Tom looked over this child with awed amazement and christened her, Carmen, in honor of her mother.

He noted the small size of the child cradled in his arms. He counted ten fingers and toes. Two eyes and a very hungry mouth. To Tom, Carmen appeared healthy, which to any new parent is a moment of great relief. He was now, after waiting so many years, going to be a father. And he knew beyond a shadow of a doubt, that he would protect her from all the evils of the world, especially when the time came, for Carmen to have children of her own.

Carmen's delightful coos soon turned as she became visibly upset. He knew at once what his crying daughter needed, warm milk or formula. The pair headed for the door, but he stopped short of opening it.

Tom realized he couldn't go shopping with baby Carmen. The grocer would ask questions. He countered that he could present Carmen as a foundling, but then foster services would surely take her. He'd again lose his Carmen. She'd come of age never knowing anything about her parents and how they loved each other, and what lengths they went to bring her into this world. Then he thought of the basement and the buried treasures that they'd discover there.

"That just won't do."

Tom at once formed a plan. They would walk the twelve blocks to the warehouse, climb into the delivery truck and drive to the country where they would start a new life together. The city, after all, was no place to raise a family.

He lay Carmen on his bed, packing a bag with clothes. He paused for a moment outside her mother's door and thanked her for everything.

Then together they scrambled down the stairs and hurried towards the door. In this haste, he failed to see the flashing red and blue lights outside his windows. As he pressed the knob the doorbell rang. In one swift movement the door opened and

Tom faced a bewildered cop on the stoop. A neighbor had phoned in a complaint about an awful smell coming from his apartment and they'd come to investigate.

The cop's bewilderment subsided instantly once the opened door emitted the rancid reek wafting from upstairs. He recognized at once the putridity of dead flesh and drew his sidearm. The neighbors crowded the sidewalk and whispers chattered amongst them, about the man who murdered his wife.

Tom stood smiling in the doorway, unflappable as always, and displayed baby Carmen to the onlookers. Then beamed with pride at the policeman and said, "We couldn't be happier. She's what my wife always wanted."

◇◇◇◇◇◇

Doubt Thou the Stars Are Fire

S.A. Cosby

◇◇◇◇◇

"What you want to drink? A rum and Coke? Vodka and cranberry? Them mumblemouth motherfuckers down at the club be drinking that pink Ciroc but I know that ain't your thing. Is it?" Amir asked. I shook my head.

"You got some Jack Daniels I'll have some of that." I said.

"Hey Shanda, get Chess a jack and Coke," he yelled into the kitchen.

"Just the Jack." I said. Amir nodded.

"Hey just the Jack. Tell you what, just bring the whole fucking bottle." He yelled. Shanda didn't respond but I was sure she heard him. A few seconds later she came sauntering out of the kitchen and handed me a heavy cut-crystal glass filled to the brim with whiskey, two lonely ice cubes dropped in there for decoration. Then she sat a mostly full fifth of Jack Daniels and a red Solo cup on the glass coffee table between me and Amir. She didn't look at me and I didn't look at her. When she walked away I stared at my drink like it was my ninth-grade algebra homework. Amir poured himself a shot.

"Five years, Chess. Man, we lucked out on that shit didn't we?" Amir said. He took his cup to the head.

"You really lucked out. You only got a year." I said. Amir nodded slowly. He was almost able to pull off that look of solemnity he was going for.

"Hey man, you didn't get the needle. Manslaughter ain't bad. And now you out. It's been what three weeks? It's like you never left," he said. I killed half my drink with one gulp. I had to keep my mouth occupied. I wonder if he noticed how tight I was gripping the glass? The whiskey burned like the devil was pissing down my throat.

"And now you the man." I wheezed after the liquor hit my belly. Amir looked around his living room. He stared at the leather living room suite and the deep pile café latte carpet. His eyes peered through the French doors that led to the patio. I watched him take in the BMW and the Mercedes sitting in his driveway. He tried to hide it, but I saw him glance toward the kitchen. Towards Shanda.

"I'm doing all right," he said finally. I took a smaller sip of my drink.

"So Boonie said you wanted to talk to me."

Amir sat forward, and I leaned back. Force of habit. If someone leans into you on the inside they either want to shank you or fuck you. Either way they looking to put something hard inside you.

"Hey man, I just wanted us to clear the air about the way things went down," he said. I sipped my drink again.

"Nothing to clear up. Your lawyer was better than mine that's all." I lied. Amir tossed his head back. His long dreads spilled across the back of the couch.

"Why did that motherfucker fight back man? We'd done that Craigslist escort thing a hundred times and nobody ever even blinked. Then that big son of a bitch wants to try and crack our skulls open."

"At the trial they said he was on meth and coke," I said.

"That nigga broke my jaw in three places. He was on some Incredible Hulk type shit." Amir said. I didn't respond. I had played that night over in my head enough when I was inside. It had been on a continuous loop the entire time I'd been in Mecklenburg State Prison. Me and Amir bursting out of the hotel room closet like thug life personified. The big naked white guy punching Shanda in the mouth. Amir getting tossed against the wall like a bag of trash. Me hitting the big guy on the back of the head with the lamp. The withering silence that fell over the room as we realized the guy was dead.

End Scene.

"It was some crazy shit," I said.

"Look man I appreciate you not snitching." Amir said. I took another big gulp of my drink. The empty glass mocked me.

"Better bite your tongue off next time he says something like that. I'm all out of ideas." I imagined it saying. I rinsed the Jack around in my mouth. I didn't snitch because in the week between beating that guy to death in the Relax Inn and the cops nabbing us we had come up with a pretty good plan. We'd just tell the cops we were partying with the dude and a fight broke out and things got out of hand. If we all stuck to the story we would have probably all gotten off with depraved indifference.

But we didn't all stick to the story did we?

I finally swallowed the whiskey. My mouth was numb. The flesh on the insides of my cheeks felt loose and gelatinous. Gelatinous. It's strange the words you pick up when you have time to read a dictionary from cover to cover.

"We were boys." I said. I tried to keep my tone nice and even.

The few people who came to see me filled me in on Amir's rise to the middle of the Richmond drug game. After he did his year he'd gotten up with Shanda. Her lawyer had kept her out of jail. She was right by his side as transitioned from being a stick-up kid to selling Special K to the club kids. Parlayed that into dealing designer drugs to hipster douchebags at the three local colleges. He'd built his shit solid enough to make some paper but fluid enough to escape the attention of Johnny Law.

"Chess you know me and Shanda that didn't start till I got out. We was never doing nothing behind you back. It just happened." He said.

"Hey, Amir, do me a favor. Don't tell me that shit okay? Nothing just happens. You didn't just look up one day and notice her fat ass all right? Don't play me like that man. Y'all together now and that's all it is. I get that. But don't tell me it just happened." I said.

Shanda came out the kitchen and went through the French doors. She had put on a leather jacket to go out into the cold February air. I watched her put a cigarette to her lips. The flame from the lighter gave her butter-pecan complexion an incandescent glow. She'd cut her hair short. When I'd gone in it had hung down to her ass. Cascading down her back like a waterfall made of shadows. That was the Shanda I knew. That was the Shanda I loved. That was the Shanda who wrote me twice a month for five years. The Shanda who dangled a carrot in front of me that kept me going in Mecklenburg.

"Maybe when you get out."

She ended all her letters like that. All one hundred and twenty of them.

"I got a job for you." Amir said. The jocularity in his voice had dried up like ditchwater in the middle of July.

"What kind of job?"

Amir stood up and went into his den. I heard him rifling through a drawer then shut it hard. When he came back out he had one of those big brown envelopes in his hand. The kind you mail documents in.

"Got some fellas outta DC coming into town tonight. They bringing me a package. Some of that good shit them Beckys over at VCU like. I can't go get it tonight, so I was gonna get you to pick it up for me." He said. Amir tossed the envelope on the coffee table. I stared at the envelope. I glanced out the patio window. Shanda was finishing her smoke.

The last letter I had received from her had been written in code. Nonsensical words and phrases that only held meaning for us. You know, the way lovers speak. She'd told me Amir beat on her. That he treated her like property. That she'd taken out a five hundred-thousand-dollar insurance policy on him. That maybe when I got out we could be together if he was out of the picture.

I stood up. I took the envelope off the table.

"I guess I'm working for you now huh?" I said. Amir frowned.

"Man don't say it like that. I owe you, Chess. You do this for me and I'll take care of you. It's the least I can do. You just pick up the package and bring it back here tomorrow." He said.

"Tomorrow?" A sheepish smile crawled across Amir's face.

"Yeah man. We going out tonight." He said.

It dawned on me what today was. I didn't keep track of holidays inside. Not Christmas. Not Thanksgiving. Least of all Valentine's Day.

Images flooded my mind that made me sick to my stomach. Amir and Shanda at some semi-fancy restaurant ordering what he thought was a good bottle of wine. Amir and Shanda riding the elevator to the top floor of the Marriott to fuck in the same two positions they did at home every three weeks. Amir laying on top of her sweating and grunting like a dying harbor seal.

That's when I knew I was going to do it.

I held out my right hand while holding the envelope in my left. Amir grabbed it and pumped it up and down twice. His grip was almost comically delicate. He'd gotten soft.

I dropped the envelope and sucker-punched him. I planted my feet and threw my hips into it. I felt a shock thrum its way up my arm as my fist connected with his cheek bone. Amir dropped to one knee. He was blinking hard and a thin stream of blood and drool poured out his mouth. I grabbed him by his dreads and dragged him to his feet.

"Five years motherfucker! How many times you fuck her in five years? A hundred? A thousand? After you sold me out." I screamed. I drove his head into the glass coffee table. It cracked but didn't break. A series of fractures raced toward its edge. I slammed his head into the table again. This time it did shatter. Glass shards rained down on his lush pile carpet. I let go of him and he crumpled to the floor.

I grabbed the Jack Daniels bottle from the wreckage of the coffee table. I gripped it by the neck and raised it above my head.

"We was boys!" I howled. I slammed the bottle into the back of his skull. It made a dull thwack!

"We was ride or die!" I said. Thwack!

"She was my girl!" I said. Thwack Thwack Thwack! When I finally dropped the bottle, it was covered in blood and Amir didn't have a face anymore. Shanda came in from the patio and closed the door behind her.

"You were supposed to wait until tonight. Come back and break in. that's why I talked him into getting you to do the pick-up. So you could get the lay of the house." She said. Her honey-coated voice melted over me. Even now with blood splattered across my face it made me shiver from the inside out.

"I...couldn't.... I couldn't let him touch you one more night. It's okay. We can make this work. Go get a blanket. We can take him out through the patio. Drop him off near the train tracks." I said. Shanda didn't speak. She headed down the hallway. I wiped my face. My hand came away red.

I heard Shanda come back into the living room. She wasn't carrying a blanket. She had a small nickel-plated .32. For a brief moment I told myself I didn't understand.

"Shanda... what are you doing?" I said even though I knew exactly what the fuck she was doing.

"You're right. We can still make it work." She said. The first shot got me in the shoulder. The hole it made in the sleeve of my t-shirt was the size of an aspirin. I stared at it, waiting for the blood to flow. I turned back to Shanda. We locked eyes.

I started for her and she shot me again. My legs disappeared from under me. I fell forward on to the remains of the coffee table.

It didn't hurt. Nothing hurt except that millisecond between seeing the gun in Shanda's hand and her pulling the trigger. I heard her talking on her cell to a 911 operator. She was explaining how her ex had broken in and beaten her husband to death and she the poor frightened waif that she was had been forced to shoot her ex. As the darkness began to

overtake me I wondered how she would explain the letters in my back pocket. All 120 of them. I'd carried them with me everywhere since I'd gotten out. Some of them even had little hearts drawn in the margins.

Ain't love grand?

◇◇◇◇◇◇

Blood Daughter

Matthew Lyons

◇◇◇◇◇◇

Stan blows up his old life with a few Facebook messages and a few cellphone photos, and after the divorce is over and he's bled dry as corn husks, he packs up his few remaining belongings in his shitty little fifth-hand Kia (the only car on Craigslist he could afford) and moves to North Garth to start rebuilding. He gets an apartment (studio), and a job (washing dishes), a new(ish) pair of sneakers and a rat in a glass case he names Salzer, after the famous German poet. He spends his first few months looking back, crying in the dark, calling his old house from grocery store parking lot payphones and hoping that Melinda doesn't pick up because they both know she's not going to let him talk to Cassie. Stan misses his daughter more than he misses the rest of his stupid old life and he tells himself that maybe that's ordinary.

Whenever his little girl answers, he never tells her it's him calling, just whispers all his secrets to her in alphabetical order and hopes she understands. When he runs out of those, he starts telling her his memories. When he was six, his dad shot himself in the garage with the Browning he brought back from Vietnam and ever since then Stan's had nightmares about red paper fans pressed against cracked window-glass. He stomped crayfish to paste by the creekside when he was a teenager. He married too young and tried to fix a broken thing with a baby.

He tells her that despite all his sins she's beautiful and she's perfect and she's all he ever wanted and that's when Melinda yanks the phone away from their daughter and screeches PERVERT!! down the line at him and then it clicks dead in his ear. The next time he tries to call, a mechanical woman tells him that number's been disconnected. He screams and smashes the receiver against the base until it comes apart in his hand and the grocery security guards have to come and drag him away off the store property.

Back home, broken and battered and hammered out of shape, he drags himself into the bathroom and scoops a handful of scummy hair from the shower drain with bloody fingers, cradles it in his palms, coos nursery rhymes to it. It's a good start. But he'll need more.

Eventually he notices there's a new waitress at the diner: her name is Alexandra and she has a green and black tattoo of a snake stretching from her right wrist all the way to the line of her jaw and she laughs at his lame dad jokes and smokes too many menthol cigarettes and carries around a five year AA token like some people carry around crucifixes. She asks him about his bandages and he makes some stupid quip, hoping she gets the message. They start to have sex a few times a week, always at her place and only ever when her boyfriend isn't home. She watches him get high sometimes and never asks why he never invites her over to his apartment.

Stan starts to plan. Stan invests in a full set of antique dental tools off eBay. Stan takes showers that last for hours, pulling out the thin hairs circling his chest and his belly and his ever-expanding bald spot and letting them collect in the drain until they just about stop up the tub before he pulls them out and adds them. Stan buys weed and sometimes coke from the other dishwasher at the diner, another down-on-his-luck case who looks like a Chad but insists everyone call him Pablo. Stan has wet dreams about his ex-wife sometimes and always calls Alexandra to apologize after. Stan starts to buy anesthetic from one of Pablo's other customers, some asshole veterinarian who can't handle his shit. Stan doesn't go in the kitchen anymore because that's her room and she needs her privacy.

Salzer's been dead under a pathetic pile of shredded paper bedding for weeks before Stan notices, and when he finally does, he just throws the whole terrarium out into the alley where it shatters and startles a homeless man so badly he never comes back around. This city is dying anyway. Stan doesn't see the poor bastard beat his retreat down and away and it's just as well because Stan wouldn't care if he did.

His apartment starts to smell like rot so he spends his whole paycheck at the Yankee Candle one Friday and congratulates himself for his ingenuity. He walls off the kitchen with broken-down boxes and cheap duct tape that doesn't tear right but gets the job done. He sings while he puts it up, The Itsy-Bitsy Spider and London Bridge and Mary Had A Little Lamb and more. He tells himself she likes it but there'll be no way to tell until he's finished and that's not going to be for a while because he has to go slowly and carefully otherwise everything's going to get fucked up and he can't let that happen.

This is too important. She's too important.

One night, laying in bed, he tells Alexandra a little bit about himself, and in return, she tells him she thinks he's the loneliest person she's ever met. She tells him about her son who lives with her parents in

TOUGH

Spokane and then he leaves because he can't handle that shit, and the next day at work she acts like nothing's wrong but he can see by the puffy glow around her eyes that she's been crying. He doesn't ask about it and she doesn't share. She doesn't answer his calls for the rest of the week either, but he's okay with that. He's got plenty of work at home to keep him occupied without having to worry about her feelings on top of all of it. He's got to focus.

Things are moving faster, now.

The next Saturday, he waits up and does lines of blow until well after midnight and then breaks into a local funeral home because those shitty Labrador painkillers he has at home aren't doing the job. He stumbles through the dark, upending chairs and caskets on his way through to the prep room and uses a screwdriver to snap the padlock off the supply locker: inside are racks of tools and rows of brown bottles with labels he only understands a little. These'll probably work. With one arm, he sweeps a whole shelf into his duffel bag for later and when a voice behind him asks

Who the hell are you? What are you doing in here?

He grabs one of the many-angled implements from the cabinet and opens the man's face with it. The sound is like a claw hammer against a steak and Stan leaves him there, crumpled on the floor in a creeping pool of his own blood.

In the bathroom of his apartment, Stan loads a pair of syringes with a mixture from the bottles and sets them on the edge of the sink while he works up the nerve. The first time he really does it, he starts small. A needle prick in the tips of his first two fingers, then he goes out to his car for the pliers while the itchy numb takes hold. He lays out paper towels all around the sink, gets a good hold, grits his teeth and yanks out one fingernail, then another. They come out with a wet sucking thwick and even through the warm embalming drug haze, the pain is exquisite, a fuzzy screaming wave that turns his whole hand into a burning, open nerve. There's not as much blood as he expected, though. He runs a cold tap over his bare fingers until it feels okay again, then he takes his ripped-free nails out to the kitchen to add.

Over the course of the next week he does the other eight, and then all ten toes, and then uses the antique bag of tools from the internet to start in on his mouth. He brings it all to the kitchen, taking his time to make sure each piece fits just so. It's only when the gaps in his smile grow wide enough to pass the neck of a bottle through that the weird, awful people at the diner start to notice. Are you okay? they ask. Do you need to talk to someone, Stan? He shrugs them all off. He's doing just fine. Every day he comes to work missing bigger clumps of hair and one time he lets slip to Pablo that he's been spending a lot of time digging for materials at the city dump. Barbed wire and medical waste. When Pablo asks him to explain a little bit more, Stan slaps him in the crotch and pretends he doesn't speak English. Pablo never talks to him again, not even when Stan comes in the next week missing the last three fingers off his left hand.

The blood seeps through the cheap vinyl off-brand bandages and gets everywhere, pattering spots on bowls and countertops and fresh napkins, but Stan insists this isn't a problem. It's no problem. He'll clean it all again, he'll scrub twice as hard. The manager sends him home and says not to come back until he's doing better. Stan asks what that means just in time to get the door shut in his face. On the way back through the parking lot, he puts a fist through the driver's side window of the manager's crappy old Buick. He stands there bleeding from both hands for a while before the idea comes to him and he starts scooping up handfuls of sea-green pebbles.

She needs eyes to see, after all.

And she always liked green. It was her favorite color.

Or was it purple?

He fills his pockets with safety glass, sure he'll find the right two somewhere in there. He's so close, now.

Back at home, Stan does all the coke he has left and it makes his brain feel like a trashcan that's on fire but if he pays attention he might be able to finish her tonight and that would make it worth all the shit and the hurt and the pain and the misery so he decides to do that: okay let's focus so we can do this come on let's fucking go. He lets himself into the kitchen through the cardboard door and goes to work, spilling his pockets all over the Formica countertop so he can find the right ones.

She waits for him at the table, hideous and cruel and nearly perfect, wrought from clumps of mottled, sticky hair and fresh stripes of leg-skin and mangled lumps of cartilage and broken bone, lashed together with tape and tight loops of wire and twine, her shape ruined humanoid, the proportions all warped and wrong. She smiles at him with his own torn-out teeth—they sit in her misshapen head glistening pearl red, arranged in as neat a row as Stan could fix them. She nods at him and he goes to work sifting through the jagged pile. The edges bite and slice into the pads of his remaining fingers, rendering the shards slick and hard to keep a hold of, but he keeps at it until he finds two that he thinks will work. He leans in and whispers to her, telling her about their angles, and when her smile spreads, he knows he made the right choice.

Stan steps in close and uses one butterflied thumb to make two little divots in her head so he can put the eyes where they need to go, but before he can place them, there's a knock at the front door.

Stannie? Alexandra calls from the other side. Stannie, are you in there? I just want to talk, please. She must have followed him home. Stannie, I'm worried about you. Nosy. She's always been nosy.

Ignore her, the creation hisses.

But Stan hesitates, stuck between the only two people left in his pathetic excuse for a life.

Open the door, Alexandra pleads. Please, Stan. I just want to help.

Give me my fucking eyes, his new child snarls.

Tears pour down Stan's face and he jams the glass into his replacement girl's makeshift skull and she shivers with pleasure, rising from her seat to meet him where he stands. Outside on the welcome mat, Alexandra's stamping her feet in frustration and calling his name, her voice swollen with sobs, but he can't hear her, now. His wretched abomination wraps him in her damp, ghastly embrace and when she squeezes it's like being devoured by knives—she shreds him apart and absorbs him, uses his parts to fortify her own, a doll of hair and meat and blood and metal. She blooms and overlaps herself, feels her father pulped inside the limits of her heinous body. She turns and tears down the fake wall, lurching toward the front of her prison, then crashes through the cheap pressboard door and onto the weeping woman she finds there, consuming her whole, the hair and steel coiling and thrashing her to red ribbons. The world beyond smells like fear, and hate, and blood, and she will devour it all, in her brutal, malignant perfection.

She opens her stolen mouth and crows to the heavens above, born to unmake the world in her image, and the gods she mocks there watch and weep and turn away to hide in their barrows. Deep inside her, as he's pulled apart and digested to slurry, Stan's last thought is of the family that left him, the world that forsook him, and in the moments before he truly becomes another part of his girl's terrible entirety, he weeps with joy.

The end has finally come.

◇◇◇◇◇◇

Leave the World a Better Place

Tom Barlow

◇◇◇◇◇

The first one went better than she could have expected. The right rifle, a .260 Remington with a Zeiss Conquest scope, which she had demanded when they divvied up her father's estate years before because she knew it had the least recoil. A comfortable place to sprawl on the floor of her van. The sun down, the parking lot of the Walmart nicely lit by halogen spotlights, her van parked in the dark beyond. A six-pack of hard lemonade in the cooler at her elbow.

Katie waited an hour for a deserving target, watching through the hole she'd bored for the scope in the back door of the van. He turned out to be a young, heavy-set man with thick black hair, most of his face obscured by the bushy beard extending well up onto his cheeks and a Red Sox baseball cap pulled down to rest on the top of his glasses. He caught her attention by scanning the parking area before reaching down between his seats, coming up with a handicapped parking pass, and clipping it onto his rear-view mirror as he pulled into a handicap spot.

She removed the plug from the lower of the two holes, the one for the barrel. Through the top opening, she located the driver's door of the car in her scope. The young man opened the door, jumped to his feet effortlessly, and shoved it shut with his hip as he took his first long strides towards the store.

She squeezed the trigger. When the rifle fired, the clap left her ears ringing. "Wear your ear protection, moron," she reminded herself, irritated.

She put the caps back in the holes in the hatch door and raised up to look through the rear window. The man lay face-down on the asphalt, blood splattered beneath him in a long arc reaching an abandoned electric cart near the curb. An elderly couple who had just exited the store had dropped to the ground with their arms over their heads. An SUV swerved around the body to grab a parking spot near the door.

Katie wrapped the rifle up in the quilt, crawled awkwardly between the seats to the front of her van and pulled away from the scene, slowly, cautiously. Her heart was beating a drum roll, and the air inside the van tasted of gunpowder.

◇◇◇◇◇◇

She finished the six-pack before she could fall asleep that evening. Her bladder woke her long before she'd rested enough though, and after the trip to the bathroom she accepted that further sleep was not possible.

She made a pot of coffee, took her blood pressure, cholesterol and pain meds, choked down a large tablespoon of peanut butter for protein, and turned on the television for some company. Deborah had always watched the news in the morning, and Katie found it a habit she didn't want to break.

A young black reporter in a sports coat too heavy for the humid summer weather stood at the edge of the Walmart parking lot, breathlessly laying out the timing and sequence of events. The actual crime scene seemed overwhelmed by the comings and goings of police, fire, Homeland Security, news cameramen, city officials, and finally, the FBI. It looked to her like a couple of acres of parking had been cordoned off with yellow tape which sagged between light poles and billowed in the breeze. Nothing he said suggested she had been seen.

Katie examined her emotions as the reporter conjectured about the origin of the fatal bullet. Guilt? Very little. The man had been able-bodied, taking up a handicap space, the kind of selfish prick that had forced her mom to walk from remote parking even when her emphysema was at its worst. Excitement? That seemed to have dissipated quickly the previous evening. Satisfaction? More like an itch that had been thoroughly scratched but would most likely return as she continued on with the plan. Pain? Still there, mostly in her ribs. She took another Percocet, wondering when her oncologist would permit her to move up to harder drugs. He seemed to be holding that out as a reward for applying for hospice.

◇◇◇◇◇◇

She didn't try to pull herself together until after lunch, in preparation for her appointment with her shrink, Eric. The mirror disappointed again. She had hair once more, but it had grown back coarse, like corn shocks after a month in the Thanksgiving display she used to hang on the front door of the urban two-story she and Deborah had shared. Her skin, once creamy, was growing increasingly transparent, so that late in the day she could track the network of veins and arteries underneath. Even the blue in her eyes seemed muddied. The only part she found pleasing was her cheekbones, much sharper after the weight loss, high enough that she looked faintly Native American.

She picked the cheeriest blouse in her closet, a polyester thant felt like silk in her hands, a fuchsia and sky-blue pattern. It momentarily improved her mood, but the adult diaper she donned brought her back down.

◇◇◇◇◇◇

"Tell me about your week," Eric said, seated beside her on his long leather couch.

Katie fixed her gaze on the fat white candle he always lit at the start of their sessions, leaned back in the couch and threw one arm on top to take pressure off her ribs. "I'm trying to do what you said—work on acceptance. Still not sleeping worth a damn. I haven't seen Deborah or Glory Beth for a month."

"How do you feel about your daughter now? Last time, you were furious about the things she said to the judge."

"I keep reminding myself she's only 15. That helps."

"You were also angry at your partner. Have you come to terms with her behavior too?"

Katie thought the word 'terms' gave her a great deal of latitude. "I'm working on that."

"Hmm," he said. "Are you still working?" He wrote something, but kept the folder tilted away from her so she couldn't see it. She figured it was something like "Agitated, fatigued."

"I had three days of temp work at a call center downtown. They didn't want me back. Evidently, I don't have a warm voice."

"How do you feel about working menial jobs? With your background in management?"

She rubbed both eyes with a pinch of her right hand. "Acceptance, right? Nobody hires cancer patients. I understand that. So I work on appreciating whatever comes along. It beats sitting at home waiting to die."

Eric wrote some more. "You've had a great deal to accept recently," he said. "Anger is normal. It might show up in ways you don't expect. Try to identify those impulses that derive from that anger and stop yourself from acting on them. In times of personal crisis, misplaced anger can drive a wedge between you and your loved ones."

Katie held back from saying the first thing that came to mind; it was already too late.

◇◇◇◇◇◇

Deborah had made her a cup of chai the afternoon of the emancipation hearing a month earlier, after their daughter Glory Beth had been finally pried away from them by Deborah's born-again bitch sister Elaine and her brother-in-law Stuart.

"You're going to stroke out if you don't watch it," Deb said, stroking Katie's neck lightly. The fingers felt like steel wool.

Katie had expected to come away from the hearing in tears, not with the seed of anger that now burned within her. But their daughter had adopted a pernicious attitude over the past two years thanks to the harping of Elaine about the ungodly relationship between Katie and Deborah. It had surfaced again that morning when Glory Beth's testimony dwelt on Deborah's licentious lifestyle. And the judge had forbidden them from even approaching their daughter for the time being, so she couldn't challenge Glory Beth's behavior.

"I told you Elaine was going to bring up that article," Katie said bitterly. She was unsure what angered her more; Deborah's repeated infidelity or the fact she had blogged it, claiming that her sexual freedom was an important example to set for their daughter, encouraging her to transcend the repressive mores of her parents' generation.

"The judge was a troglodyte," Deb replied. "Sometimes you just have to make a stand, even if it causes you pain in the short run." When she tried to put her arm around Katie she slapped it away.

"I can't stand to have this argument ever again. I'm moving out."

"We've been together almost twenty years. You can't just throw that away."

"As far as I can tell, you throw it away every time you walk out of here to meet your lovers."

◇◇◇◇◇◇

Katie still read the newspaper, curious about the future despite her prognosis. Daily delivery was one of the first things she'd arranged when she moved into the tiny efficiency apartment in a neighborhood quickly on its way to becoming a barrio for immigrants from Central America. She circled an article in the Metro section about a Tom Abalo, a forty-year-old brick mason who had just been arrested for driving drunk for the tenth time. This time he'd clipped a boy on a bicycle who ended up losing a leg. Appallingly, Abalo was free on bail, even though he'd been forbidden from driving since his fourth conviction.

He still had a land line, so she was able to bring up his address from the White Pages. Googling his name provided a photo of him with a couple of proud homeowners posed in front of their new brick patio.

Luckily, her beat up van, which she and Deb had kept only because it was handy for hauling Deb's pottery to weekend shows, did not look out of place in Abalo's neighborhood, where virtually every driveway sported a panel van advertising a construction or repair service. She parked down the street where she had a clear view of his house from the floor of the van. The sun had set, and despite the heat, she was cold at her core, so she snuggled into the sleeping bag they had bought for the women's retreat where Deb's infidelity had found its first legs.

She put a stick of gum in her mouth and waited; although she had zero appetite, the chewing gave her the illusion of eating, and she was content with illusion at the moment. With all the opiates, food lost velocity in her colon and could be coaxed into passing through with only the greatest difficulty.

While there were no streetlights in this development, many of the houses had gas lights shining on their sidewalks, and the soft glow gave just enough illumination to frame anyone coming out of a house. She waited, and waited, until at just after 10:00 p.m. when Abalo walked out of his house, jumped in the truck in the driveway, and backed out. Katie started the van. When the truck passed her, she followed from a distance. As she expected, he drove less than a mile to a bar in a strip mall on Westerville Road, Jack's Lounge.

She figured he was there for quite a spell, so she took the opportunity to hit the McDonald's down the road to change diapers and was back on post, parked in the lot of a closed window repair shop across the road, when he came out of the bar at 1:00 a.m. He was in the company of two other drunks, but fortunately they peeled off, got in another pickup and left before Abalo, walking unsteadily, reached his. The shot was a piece of cake, although the sound echoed for a couple of seconds from the glass storefronts of the strip mall.

She wove her way home via back roads to avoid any traffic cams and arrived by 1:30 a.m. Her ribs were aching brutally thanks to the hours spent on the hard floor of the van, but the sense of retribution made the pain endurable.

◇◇◇◇◇◇

She had fallen into a restless sleep on her futon late that morning when the doorbell rang. She'd told no one except her ex-boss Bev Crosley where she was living, so she was expecting her when she opened the door. Only at the last moment did she think to wonder if it could be a cop, a bit of obliviousness that surprised her.

However, it was neither. Instead, there stood Deborah holding a fruit bouquet of chocolate-dipped prunes. There was no contrition on the woman's face, but Katie couldn't remember ever seeing her ex-wife contrite. Or embarrassed, for that matter. She wore the faint smile she always did, like she saw something everyone else didn't.

She stepped aside so Deb could enter. She'd forgotten already how much taller her ex was than her, willowy, all the way to hair which moved like sea grass in the lightest of breezes. She had always loved running her fingers through Deb's hair.

Deb placed the bouquet on the counter that divided the living room from the kitchen. "These still work on your constipation?"

"There's such a thing as knowing one another too well," Katie said, taking a seat on one of her bar stools. "What are you doing here? And how did you find me?"

Deb took a seat on the other bar stool, so that their knees almost touched. Katie scooted back.

"I called Bev. She's worried about you, and so am I. I'm hoping to convince you to move back home.

It's like a house full of ghosts back there, and I miss you like crazy."

"Too late," Katie said. "I've moved on. You should too."

"Moved on to what? An apartment the size of a closet? More painkillers? Kid, we've been through too much together to watch you die alone. To hell with Glory Beth; give her another month with the God Squad and she'll come begging us to let her return."

"It's not that, and you know it," Katie said, shoving the bouquet further away; the smell was nause-ating her. "I only stayed with you for the last two years for Glory Beth's sake. Since you starting cheating."

"I told you right up front what I was doing, as you'll remember. I thought maybe now, when you're close to, you know, you'd see how silly it is to let other people stand in the way of living life on your terms. But I'll tell you what; you come back, I'll remain faithful. If that's what it takes."

"Which will make me just what you despise, right? The person who takes away your freedom? No thanks."

"So what are you going to do?" Deb's cheeks were flushed, a sign Katie had long recognized as a precursor to an angry outburst. "Hole up here until you die? For Christ's sake, there's not even anyone to find the body. You could lay here until you rot before someone knows you've passed."

"I'm working on a project," Katie said. "Believe me, there will be plenty of people know when I die."

"I don't like the sound of that."

"Meditate on this. I don't want you. I don't need you. Go and sleep with anybody you want. Be free." She waved her hand toward the door.

Deb stood, frowned, shook her head. "You poor girl. Don't be afraid to call me when you need me. And you will." She left without a backward glance.

◇◇◇◇◇◇

On the news that evening the murder was the lead story; given the history of the victim, there was a hint of schadenfreude in the reporter's voice. Fortunately, there was still no mention of a witness, although the reporter conjectured that the shots might have come from a van or SUV. They did suggest a possible link with the Walmart shooting.

She had expected a race between her mortality and discovery, so she wasn't all that worried that they might have pieced together a bit of the plan. The day of her death was still in her control.

The next morning, though, she woke exhausted, only then realizing she had forgotten to eat the day before. With disgust, she ate a few of the prunes from the bouquet and rinsed them down with a bottle of Ensure. It was mid-afternoon before she had the energy to browse for her next victim.

It didn't take long. Scott Van Driesen, once a wide receiver for the local university, had been caught eleven years earlier raping a coed at knife point. Since his release from prison two months before, two women had been raped by a man match- ing his description and method. However, the Colum- bus Dispatch reported that the woman Van Driesen was living with, Polly Bender, who had been one of his guards in prison, insisted he'd been home with her both nights. Caught by the photographer, Van Driesen had given the most appallingly smug smile when asked if he did it.

◇◇◇◇◇◇

Bender had a house in the country twenty miles west of Columbus, which magnified the difficulty. Katie assumed the sheriff's department was going to keep an eye on him, although she doubted they had the manpower to watch him around the clock. The night was once again going to be her friend.

She studied the layout on Google Earth. The house was surrounded by cornfields, the nearest neighbor a quarter-mile away. There was a lane a hundred yards to the west of the house to allow tractor access to the corn fields. Since the August heat had baked the ground dry, she presumed she could park there.

She had never made a Molotov cocktail before, but she remembered the olive oil vases that had been Deb's obsession for a while, until she discovered they were too brittle. Waiting until Deb was at work, she returned to the two-story long enough to snatch one that would hold a quart of gasoline. It was shaped like an acorn squash, easy for her to throw.

The lane through the corn was indeed bone dry; she was able to back well away from the road at 3:00 a.m. the next morning. She made her way on foot down a row of corn toward the house, the rifle over her shoulder, the gas bomb in her left hand. She nicked her earlobe on a corn leaf and it began to drip blood, but the pain disappeared into that of her ribs.

She stopped at the border between corn and lawn, laid the rifle down, and pulled out the lighter she'd brought from home, the one she used to fire up the medical marijuana that had proven so useless. She played out the steps in her mind, took a deep breath and walked quickly to the house. There she lit the fuse and, with all her remaining strength, threw it through the picture window of the living room.

As flames lit the interior of the house, she dashed back to the corn, dropped to the ground, picked up the rifle and sighted on the front door.

She was almost too slow when the two of them exited instead through the kitchen door on her side of the building. She quickly sighted on Van Driesen as he turned on the outside faucet and fumbled with the hose curled at his foot. She aimed for his back, but hit him in the head instead.

To her surprise, Bender, an older, obese woman, didn't run; instead, unthinkably, she ran in Katie's direction, shrieking. She waited as long as she could for the woman to come to her senses before dropping her with a shot to the chest only ten yards from her sniper's nest.

The fire department responded so rapidly she had to wait for them to pass by before pulling her car out of the corn and speeding away.

◇◇◇◇◇◇

Every time she started to drift into sleep, Van Driesen's face, at the moment of impact, came back to her. She had thought her heart adamantine, but apparently she had a bit of work yet to do to purge herself of sentiment. And she felt repentant about Bender. The woman had been a liar and a fool but didn't deserve to die for such scum.

To her surprise, the sheriff of Sheridan County was quite open on TV that morning about what the Ohio Bureau of Criminal Investigation had found on the scene. They had recovered a shoe print from where she had approached the house, a tire print from where she parked, and a blood sample from the corn leaf on which she had cut her ear. Luckily, she was sure her DNA was not in any police database. They had matched the bullets in all three killings, though, and the television people were barely able to disguise their delight at having a serial killer to draw viewership. Even more so as the BCI had concluded from the footprint that the perp was a woman.

Katie walked into the bedroom and grabbed her father's Glock, tucked it into her waistband.

◇◇◇◇◇◇

"Tell me about Glory Beth," Eric had asked during her first visit six months earlier.

"She's precocious," Katie said. "She should be, given the amount we spent on sperm."

"And your partner? Is she smart too?"

"Very much so. It's gotten so sometimes I have trouble following their conversations."

"That must be annoying, since you were the birth mother."

"I guess so. Sometimes I get the sense that Glory Beth sees Deborah as her mother, or maybe her father, or both, while I'm something else. I can't put my finger on what. A wicked aunt, maybe?"

"From what you've told me about your partner, she sounds like a person who makes people earn her respect."

"Oh, that's true. She can be downright rude to people. But not to Glory Beth. She can do no wrong in Deb's eyes."

"But not in yours."

"I can tell the girl is going to break my heart. I just don't know how."

"Did you ever consider that your ambivalent feelings about your daughter might be in part transference of your feelings about Deb?"

Katie had sat quietly mulling this over for several minutes, until the silence grew too oppressive. "How much am I paying you for this bullshit?"

◇◇◇◇◇◇

She had intended to complete the plot in the morning, before the lawyers trickled off to court, but her ribs kept her up late, until she took an extra couple of Percocet. They left her drowsy until 11 a.m., and by the time she showered, dressed, and wrote out her confession, it was early afternoon.

The traffic was one thing she was not going to miss, she thought as she fought her way downtown. Luckily, the parking garage across from the firm where Deb worked had several open handicapped slots on the ground floor. Ironically, it had been Deb who convinced her to get a script for a handicapped mirror hanger.

She laid the rifle on the passenger seat, where the police were sure to find it, and used her phone to email her confession to them. She adjusted the Glock in the small of her back.

As she rode the elevator to the fourth floor of the building across the street, she realized that the outfit she was wearing, the mint-green taffeta blouse, the tailored slacks, the melon blazer, the Blahnik flats, had been bought for her by Deb. That was a mistake, but she was too far into it to return home and change.

She had never cared for the firm's receptionist, Astana Poole, a woman who had a way of looking at her that she found demeaning, unsure it if was personal or simply a strategy to put clients in their proper place, subordinate to their attorneys. Therefore, she wasn't afraid to pull the pistol as she walked up to her. The waiting area was otherwise unoccupied.

"What in the world?" Poole said, finger poised above her phone.

"Before you call 9-1-1, call Deb. Tell her I'm waiting for her. Don't tell her any more than that."

Poole, hands shaking, pressed Deborah's extension. Katie couldn't hear her answer, since Poole was wearing a headset, but was content that the woman did just as she instructed.

"Now call the cops."

Poole, puzzlement on her face, punched the number. When the police answered, she identified herself, gave the address, and said, "We have a woman in the lobby named Katie Frank holding me at gunpoint. I think she means to kill Deborah Kline, one of our attorneys."

When Poole began nodding, and Katie said, "That's enough. Hang up."

She did so. "Please don't kill me."

"You do what I tell you, you'll walk away from this. Understand?"

Poole nodded. Katie could smell the odor of urine wafting across the room, and was pretty sure her diaper was dry.

Just then, Deb came around the corner, saw the setup, and stopped. "What the hell are you doing?"

"You and I have some unfinished business." She swung the gun around to point at her ex.

"What? You're going to kill me now? Are you really that angry?"

"You cost me my daughter. Shouldn't I be?"

Deb wrapped her arms across her chest. "Elaine took Glory Beth from us. You know that."

Katie's arm was trembling. "But you provided the ammunition. It's you that deserves the punishment."

"So that's why you're going to kill me. To punish me for losing Glory Beth."

"Who said I was going to kill you? I've done far worse. I hope you enjoy going through the rest of your life known as the wife of a serial killer."

Deb was silent for a long moment. "It was you? That shot those people? That was your project?"

Katie heard Poole gasp. In the distance, she could also hear a siren. "The guidance counselor in my high school asked me once what I was going to do to leave the world a better place. I figure I've done my bit."

"I never knew you had such cruelty in you," Deb said. Katie could see the tears coursing down her cheeks.

"Cruel? You haven't seen anything yet. When you think of me, I don't want you dredging up sweet memories, so here's my last gift. I want you to remember me just like this."

And with that, she raised the gun to her temple and fired.

◇◇◇◇◇◇

Ruby Behemoth

(opening excerpt)

Court Merrigan

◇◇◇◇◇◇

Ruby Hix stood outside the gates of the Women's Penitentiary in Chowchilla, California. Looked up and down the dusty highway for Ivy but Ivy was not there.

She waited an hour outside the gates, as long as the guards would let her , then walked down to the bus stop. Caught the 9303 bus down to Fresno. Fresno hadn't changed much in these seven years and six months. Eleven city blocks to Gallo Union Pawn Shop, blinking back all the light and life and noise of the hot summer streets. A dull gnawing in her lower belly reminded her she needed tampons, pronto. She stepped into the sudden cool darkness of the shop and walked down an aisle of pawned leather jackets breathing in the scent of thwarted men. A couple other patrons noticed her two hundred and twenty ropy pounds of coiled energy and decided to look elsewhere..

"I help you?" the clerk asked, keeping his hands out of sight.

"That baton there," Ruby said, throwing the grip bag up on the counter. "It work?"

The clerk slid open the glass, removed the squat extendable baton from the shelf, the kind cops keep strapped to their gun belts. "You tell me," he said, and handed it across the counter.

Ruby hefted the baton in her hand. The balance felt right. Snapped her wrist and the baton snicked out to full length with a soft hiss, metal gleaming dull in the light. She took a few experimental swings, cutting the air with a stroke born of the mystery of speed. Another swing, another. She knew just what these cuts could do to soft flesh and brittle bone.

Then she tapped the tip against the heel of her palm. The shaft collapsed inside the handle. She rolled it over in her palm. Someone had scritched "PRATHER" in the leather cover on the handle.

"Who's Prather?" she asked.

"You serious?"

"I could be."

The clerk cocked his head. "You're Ruby Hix, ain't you?"

Ruby shrugged.

"Linda talks about you. Linda Patrecho. Said you helped her out with the Featherwoods."

"I did what I said I would."

"Yeah. She told me that, too."

"How much for the baton?"

The clerk shook his head. "For you? Free. Linda Patrecho's my cousin."

The word "free" washed over Ruby like a benediction. Seven years and six months she worked every shitty trusty job they'd give her back in Chowchilla, swabbing toilets, washing dishes, pressing laundry. Came away with a grand total of $477.18.

"Thank you," Ruby said.

"De nada." Linda Patrecho's cousin leaned over the counter, voice gone conspiratorial. "Listen," he said. "There's work. If you want it."

"No," Ruby says. "No more work."

"Linda said you wanted to go straight. Won't last, you know." The clerk straightened behind the counter, nudged the baton across the counter. "You sure as hell won't get much done with this stick."

"You might be surprised," Ruby said.

◇◇◇◇◇◇

Ruby walked five blocks down to the Ralph's. She stood in the cereal aisle a long time. The last time she'd been here in this Ralph's it was with Ivy, and the store manager had to call out security and a check-out boy with a broom to clean up their mess at the tail end of Ruby's attempt to coax her big sister down off a two-week bender.

"They're going to call the cops," Ruby said desperately, picking herself up from a pile of Honey Nut Cheerios boxes.

"I hope they do!" Ivy screamed. "I hope they fucking cart you away!"

Ruby held out a hand. "Just come on," she said. "I know you don't mean that. Come with me. I'm going to help you."

Ivy's eyes were so dilated Ruby could see the back of her skull. She was shivering and her T-shirt was dirty. She skittered backward when Ruby grabbed for her wrist.

"You can't help me," Ivy said. "You can't do shit for me." Turned and galloped for the exit.

"Fuck you too, then!" Ruby shouted at her sister's retreating back.

Then a sprinting security guard tackled Ruby and by the time she got untangled from his beefy grip and nacho breath Ivy was long gone.

Ruby searched for Ivy for three December days smack in the middle of Fresno's most frigid cold snap in fifty years, living on Butterfingers and battery-acid gas-station coffee, sleeping in the puke-yellow '79 Datsun she hadn't insured in over a year that featured four bald tires and one working heater vent, haunting Fresno's back alleys with a baton in her hand.

She didn't find Ivy. Instead she got harassed by some suit downtown. The suit got a few less teeth and a squashed nut sack, Ruby got arrested, the suit got a lawyer, and Ruby got seven-to-nine. The next time she saw Ivy it was through prison plexi-glass, too late for tears.

Ache in her lower belly worsening, Ruby strode the fluorescent aisles of Ralph's in a daze at the abundance. About seven hundred items to crave . A bag of marshmallows, a five-pound sack of hot dogs, toffee ice cream bars, a pair of leather work boots especially caught her eye. But all she put in her in basket was a pack of off-brand unscented tampons, a jar of dill pickles and a bottle of barbecue sauce. These last two she'd craved endlessly back in Chow-chilla. At the check-out she menaced the cashier with a hard stare,. In prison they'd short you on taters and beans if you didn't keep a careful watch. She'd once seen a trusty cook take a fork in the cheek over a scanty ladle of beans.

Ruby headed straight to the ladies room with her purchases and did her best to get comfort-able on her first enclosed privy in seven years and six months. Grunted with pleasure at this first red-tinged piss in the free world, then fumbled around with the slick tampon. Surpassing strange to slip it inside herself. Been a long while. In prison they only issued pads, the thin kind with no adhesive wings, and then only half a dozen at a go. Ruby bled pretty heavily and rationing out those half dozen little pads out was an impossibility. So she'd have to buy extra at the commissary, cursing every dollar they ticked off her meager account. So she sat a moment longer on the toilet, looking at the little string dangling between her big thighs. Felt a whole lot like freedom.

Thirty-one years old and so far life had pinballed Ruby Hix from one institution to the next trailer park. She took her time.

On the way out, Ruby passed by the Play Center. A gaggle of kids surrounded a chubby boy cowering on a Garfield tea cup.

"Fatty McBlatty! Fatty McBlatty!" the kids chanted at the chubby boy, his lip atremble, near tears.

Ruby Hix remembered her own nickname. She shoved the bullies aside, sent them crying for their mommies.

"You all right?" she asked the chubby boy.

The boy looked up and down her bulk. Pulled a face. "Leave me alone, fatso," he said. Slipped off the Garfield teacup and ran away.

◇◇◇◇◇◇

In Chowchilla Ruby volunteered for every work detail they had, eventually working her way up to trusty status and the floor-waxing crew. To spend a dime felt like robbing the future so she went without everything she could. A pillow was seven bucks at the commissary (85 hours of labor). An extra blanket, eleven (157 hours). The ticket lady at the Greyhound station had to pry the eighty-three dollars (1185 hours) for a ticket to Barstow out of her palm.

In the waiting room Ruby ran a thick stream of barbecue sauce over a dill pickle, slippery in her fingers. More delicious than she could have believed, starbursts of flavor a supernova on her tongue.

She ate half a dozen pickles, barely breathing, then licked her fingers clean. All the while hoping, somehow, that Ivy would show. Ivy did not show. On the TV Bruce Jenner was calling himself "Caitlyn" and the host kept asking why.

"Why the fuck not?" Ruby said out loud. Her fellow passengers looked away.

She went to the bathroom and locked the door and stood in front of the mirror, practicing with the baton. The trick was to get it out of your pocket and extended in one fluid motion, ready to strike. Fifty or so practice flicks in, she started to get the old feel back.

The bus departed Fresno at 10:10PM. Wedged into a seat two sizes too small for her frame, Ruby was plenty glad to pass the lion's share of California in the dark. Fuck this state and the seven years and six months it'd stolen from her. She sat in the aisle seat, ignoring the window, dipping dill pickles in barbecue sauce. After a time the motion of the bus swayed her to sleep. She dreamed of Ivy and pickle juice swimming pools.

When she woke it was dawn in Barstow and her mouth tasted of salt. Someone had stolen her pickle jar. She filed out of the bus with the other passengers and in the terminal scanned the crowd with no actual hope and Ivy was not there.

She strapped her black sling bag over a shoulder and headed out of the station, ignoring the cabbies. Like she'd spend that kind of dough on a cab, for Chrissakes. All she bought was a bottle of Mountain Dew to wash the salt taste out of her mouth. It was just past nine AM but already sweltering here in the desert.

In the library at Chowchilla Ruby had memorized a map of Barstow. The return address on Ivy's last letter read #32 at the Coach Lamp Trailer Court and Ruby knew just how to get there. She walked at an unhurried pace. In that last letter Ivy mentioned working steady. Middle of the day like this, maybe nobody would be home. Maybe Ivy occupied a position of some importance somewhere. Maybe that's why she hadn't been there at the prison gates, or up for a visit the whole last five years of Ruby's spit.

Ruby's feet soon ached on the uneven cement and in the oven of desert heat and she paused to rest in what meager shade the Barstow streets offered. That Shawshank Redemption bullshit was even more bullshit than she'd thought back in Chowchilla. The world hadn't gone and gotten itself in a big damn hurry. To Ruby it seemed more like everything moved in a gel of slow motion, clear and bright and wondrous, a passing red-and-white Budweiser truck, a little girl on a pink-frilled bike, glazed donuts sweating in a bakery window.

Midday had come and gone by the time Ruby arrived at the Coach Lamp Trailer Court. One of those rural ghettos the news shows ignore, pay-by-the-week trailers, some with the siding ripped away in patches to expose rows of pink insulation, others with plywood nailed over windows, yet others with tires on the roof.. Ruby walked down the hot gravel lanes to #32. A brown-and-white striped single-wide, no car out front, no name on the mailbox, railroad ties reeking of creosote stacked up to the door to form a stairway. A half- collapsed knee-high white plastic fence shielded a patch of dead grass with a hose coiled up in it. She turned on a tap and let the hot water ran out of the hose before slaking her thirst with long gulps, splattering the dust on her boots. Then someone swung the door open. Ruby dropped the hose.

Not Ivy. A little boy.

◇◇◇◇◇◇

The little boy had dark olive skin and straw-black hair and a snotty nose and a pair of iridescent violet eyes, blinking at her. Ruby had to look deep to believe those eyes were real. They were. Other-worldly, but real. The boy also had Ivy's hooked nose and bangs that curled a notch above his eyebrows, just so. It required no imagination, none, to know whose child this was.

"Aunt Ruby?" he said, ending any more suspense on the point.

Ruby dropped to one knee to get down to the little boy's level and also so she wouldn't lose her balance. "I'm Ruby," she said, not quite able to append the title of "aunt" to herself.

The boy responded by throwing his arms around her neck, snotty nose pressed against her cheek. The first human being to touch her in affection in seven years and six months and Ruby enveloped the child in her hefty arms and squeezed just as long as the boy would let her.

"You got a name, big guy?" Ruby asked, relinquishing her grip but hanging onto the boy's shoulders.

"I'm Leo," the boy said, voice cracking with tiny earnestness.

"Leo the lion, huh?"

Leo's face brightened with pure pleasure. "Mama says the same thing."

"I bet she does," she said. When they were girls, Ivy had toted that stuffed lion doll across half the country. Yellow-maned and snaggle-toothed. Named Leo. Leo the lion. "So is your mama home?"

Before the boy could answer footsteps clattered from the back to answer for him. Ruby stood, runnels of sweat running down the small of her back. Ivy, all right, but shrunk down to an altogether different person. Once upon a time, schoolgirl days, Ivy had been full-figured. A little pudgy, even. Now she was a waif. Wrists like twigs. Hair so thin you could see her ears through the strands. Peachy arm hair blossomed on her forearms and her collarbones beneath a cheap T-shirt looked about to bust through her skin. Perched in the doorway like dandelion fuzz.

Look at the Hix girls. Come to bad ends, the both of them. Just like Mrs. Custer back at Little Lake Agnes School predicted.

But fuck Mrs. Custer. Ruby dropped her grip bag and wrapped her arms around her big sister's neck.

"Heya, Banana Bean," she said.

◇◇◇◇◇◇

Ivy turned on Leo's cartoons and while the boy sat on the floor clutching a stained pillow the two sisters stood in the kitchen and talked.

"Why didn't you tell me about him?" Ruby asked.

"I don't know!" Ivy said. "I don't know. How you are, I guess. You worry. I didn't want you to worry."

"When did this happen? How old is he?"

"Seven. Well, six and a half."

"So that's why you didn't come to see me the last half of my spit."

"It was bad, Moon Pie. You don't understand."

Strange, so strange to hear that pet name again. "You don't suppose I maybe would've like to see him?" Ruby said softly.

Ivy shook her head. "I know that. It ain't about that."

"What's it about, then?"

"You know how it is when you go up there, all them forms you got to fill out. Background check and all. I was worried if I showed up there, they'd. . .take him."

"As bad as that, huh?"

"It was. For a while."

"Jesus. What have you been doing since I been gone? Is that why you're living in fucking Barstow?"

Ivy shook her head. "It's better than it was."

"But you still couldn't come up to see me?"

"By then Brett didn't want me to. He says he won't go within a hundred miles of a prison if he can help it and he sure wasn't going to drive me to one."

"Tell me this Brett is Leo's father."

Ivy looked away. "No. I can't tell you that."

"Then I don't see what say he gets a say in where you go and don't go."

"This is his house, Moon Pie. His car. He took us in, me and Leo both. We had to have somewhere to go."

Ruby looked around the shabby trailer. "Looks like he's a real prince."

"Oh, Ruby. You should've seen him up there. Singing."

"Singing."

"He was a real rock n' roll singer, Moon Pie. Had a band and toured and everything."

"Made a real mint at it, I can see."

"Not everything's about money, you know."

"Aren't rock stars supposed to die young?"

"Ah, Christ, Moon Pie." She giggled. "You haven't changed a damn bit."

"Were you expecting me to?"

"No."

"All right then. So what happened to you working steady? Like you said in your letter?"

Ivy shrugged. "I was. At the Family Dollar. Now I'm not."

"This just gets better and better. Let me guess. Your rock star didn't like you working?"

Ivy shook her head. "No."

"I knew it. They're all the same, these assholes. Everywhere you go, they're all the same."

"Brett says to in order to get a paycheck you got to let them track you. Social security number and address and all? Even computers and drones, Brett says."

"So? It's a job. They got to know something about you."

"Brett don't want no one tracking him. He worries about it all the time." Ivy nibbled her fingers. "He don't even like me leaving the house."

"Shit."

"You should've seen the fit he pitched when I even wrote you the one letter telling you we were here in Barstow."

"Who's this asshole think he is? CIA?" She looked over at Leo at his cartoons. "So he's not a rock star anymore?"

"Not really."

"What's he do then?"

"Oh, you know. This and that. For people he met on the road, you know."

"On the road."

"You know. When he was touring."

"Right. Fucking drugs, isn't it. Ivy? Jesus Christ. Don't tell me he's running fucking guns."

"No!"

"Then it's drugs. He runs drugs."

"He doesn't sell them, Moon Pie. He's just a courier. Back and forth. That's why we live here. All the interstates. He keeps it to small-time stuff, you know? Keeps us in bread."

"So what's his plan? Keep you locked up forever so he can be a piss-ant in the middle of nowhere for the cartels?"

"Not the cartels."

"Who then?"

"Russians."

"Boy, Ivy, this story just never stops getting better, does it?"

"I had to go somewhere, Moon Pie. So this is where I went. Anyway, he worries about us."

"Yeah. I bet. I just bet he's got you and little Leo's best interests right at the tippy top of his mind." Ruby looked out at Leo, sitting cross-legged about three feet from the TV. "So what happened to Leo's real daddy?"

"Gone."

"For good?"

"I see him every now and again. I never know when."

"So after Leo's daddy took off you you took up with this asshole here."

"Among others." Ivy tugged a Red Apple out of the pack, blew a hard wreath of smoke around her face.

"You shouldn't smoke around him, you know." Ruby juts a chin toward Leo at the TV.

"You're right, you're right." Ivy stabbed out the smoke after one long last drag. "What'd you want me to do, Ruby? Leave California?"

"What's that supposed to mean?"

"You know what I mean. I couldn't leave you behind."

"Don't throw that in my face! Don't."

"I'm not throwing it. I'm telling you what's true. I'm telling you why I ended up here. In this shithole. With this asshole."

Ruby put her hands on her hips. Felt it all flowing out of her.

"Ah, hell, Banana Bean," she said. "You're right. I'm sorry. It is so good to see you."

"I'm just doing what I have to, Ruby."

"I know."

"You know how they are."

"Yeah. I know exactly how they are. I also know you don't have to do nothing. Not from now on. And I tell you what. I'm going to get you out of here. Away from this asshole. Out of this shithole."

She hugged her waifish and cigarette-reeking sister, feeling every bone all down Ivy's back. So delicate she looked built of fish bones.

"Hey," Ruby said, "at least you stuck with him, huh? More than we can say for mama."

They released each other. Ivy's eyes were wet and she wiped at her cheeks. "Do you ever think about her, Moon Pie?" she asked.

"Mama?"

"Yeah."

Ruby snorted. "You think she ever thinks about us?"

"I like to think so."

"Why? So you can slap her face if she ever showed it around here?"

"Ruby!"

"I mean it. She never gave a fuck about us, Banana Bean."

"You don't know that."

"How do I not know that? She was out the door five minutes after they snipped my umbilical cord."

"That's just what Daddy used to say."

"Yeah, well, Daddy was there, wasn't he? Why are we talking about Mama, Banana Bean?"

Ivy smiled. "Maybe she really was a secret agent."

Ivy used to make up stories to tell Ruby about Mama, back in that house in Wyoming. That she was a secret agent dueling with Chinese, or an adventurer hacking her way on a secret mission through a distant dark jungle, or a cowgirl riding a lonesome range. All the stories with the same origin and ending: Mama had no choice but to go, to save their lives, to keep them safe, to fulfill a grand destiny.

"I got to hit the head," Ruby said, and pushed past Ivy.

In the bathroom Ruby inserted a fresh tampon, counted how many she had left. Not enough. Then she stuck her face in the crook of her elbow, to stifle the sobs at this squalid homecoming.

◇◇◇◇◇◇

Ruby sat cross-legged on the floor watching Scooby-Doo with Leo curled up on her lap when the screen door slammed and Leo flinched and Ruby could feel his whole little body tense up.

"Ivy!" yelled the man who stumbled through the doorway. "Ivy!"

Brett stumbled in the door in a stained black leather jacket and floppy hair and a miasma of beer. He toted a sixer of Mickey's looped around one finger and a battered guitar case. He set both on the counter and cracked himself a beer, narrowed eyes hard on Ruby. Ivy sidled up next to him, fawning-like. Made Ruby want to puke, the way her sister minced up to him like he was some kind of conquering hero when it looked to Ruby like he hadn't conquered anything more than a few innocent cans of beer.

Same old story. Ivy drew herself to men such as this like a a bad habit. Daddy issues.

Ruby gently slid Leo off her lap and stood. She thought Leo would stay with Scooby-Doo but he followed her instead. Brett wrapped an arm around Ivy and ignored them.

"I'm about to hit it big-time, baby," he said to Ivy.

"Oh?" Ivy said.

"That's right." He drummed his fingers on the old guitar case. "You got no idea, baby."

"That's good, honey. That's real good."

"You goddamn right it is." He turned and gave Ruby the old once-over, not all that different from the one the toughs liked to put on back in the yard at Chowchilla. "This the jailbird little sister, huh?"

"This is Ruby," Ivy said.

"Hi, Brett," Ruby said, and stuck out a hand.

Brett considered her hand. Took a long pull of Mickey's, set the can down, and then took Ruby's hand.

"Be damned, girl," he said. "You sure you been in lockup and not in the fitness protection program?"

"Brett!" Ivy said.

"What?" Brett said, and slugged more beer. "I'm just saying."

Ruby didn't say anything. Leo clung to her substantial leg.

"Leo, honey," Ivy said. "Go back to your cartoons, huh?"

"But, moooom ..."

"Just do it, sugar. Please."

Leo reluctantly tore himself away from his aunt and back to the cartoons. Brett planted himself on a stool. Polished off the Mickey's. Ivy unringed him another and he popped the tab. Pushed the remainders towards Ruby.

"Beer?" he asked.

"No thanks," Ruby said.

"Why not? Better than that hooch they got up in the clink."

"I didn't drink there, either."

"Suit yourself. I don't trust a man who won't have a drink with me but I guess in your case I'll make an exception."

"Jesus Christ, Brett," Ivy said, pushing away from him.

"What? What? I'm just fucking with her. She's used to that, ain't you? Ruby? Ain't you? Up where you came from they fuck with you all the time, don't they?"

"Sure."

"Course, that ain't all you fuck with, is it."

"Brett, would you watch your mouth?" Ivy said. "Leo's right there."

"Don't push me, woman," Brett said. "I got a hundred places I could go." But as he talked he kept a steady drunken eye on Ruby. "I heard," he said, "that you all are a bunch of rug munchers up there. Bet it was one a hell of a scene, huh? All you rug munchers up there. Just going at it." He stuck out his tongue and flicked the naked air to a sloppy flapping sound. "That true? Ruby? That true? You a rug muncher, Ruby?"

"No," Ruby said.

"Well, you'll have to pardon me. Ivy here's never much talked about you. I guess that's understandable enough."

"Brett. . ." Ivy said again.

Brett ignored her. "How long were you upstate, little sister?"

"Seven years," Ruby said. "Seven years and six months."

"Long stretch. Out on parole?"

"No. I wouldn't take none of that. I did my full spit. That way I owe 'em nothing."

"I'd say that was smart except for the fact that you ended up there in the first place." He tapped the briefcase on the counter with the flat of his hand. "Me, I ain't been caught at nothing. Ain't planning on it, neither." He staggered a little on his stool, caught himself from falling over.

"Good for you."

"Yeah. Good for me. Well, at least you ain't one of them bull dykes. One less character defect you got. I suspect you got several you're not telling me about, though. Hell, if I'd have known my sweet Ivy here had a jailbird for a sister, I might never have took up with her in the first place." He wrapped an arm back around Ivy. "Man like me can't afford to keep company with someone who'll rat on anyone to keep from going back inside."

"I ain't a rat," Ruby said.

"Not yet you're not. But I know you ex-cons will do just about anything from having to pull another stretch. Wait until they pull you over for a busted headlight and start asking you hard questions and talking about sending you back to the cage with the rug munchers and you just think to yourself, what, what, what can I give them." Brett swigged hard on his beer. "What or who."

"I'm free. I ain't got to beg to no one."

"Sure you are. Bet you were telling yourself right up until they threw you in the back of the police cruiser last time, too, huh?" He squeezed Ivy tighter to his side. "Like I say, the way I see it, the trouble ain't what you did. It's that you got caught for it."

"I got caught because the man I did it to couldn't walk away from it," Ruby said.

"Whatever, little sister." Brett looked back at Ivy. "She can stay one night. That's it. One night. Then jailbird here hits the fucking bricks. I ain't having no ex-con hanging around this place."

"All right, sugar," Ivy said. "All right."

"I want her to say longer!" came a squeaky and quavering voice.

No one had noticed how little Leo had sneaked away from Scooby-Doo and back into the adult conversation. But now there he stood, plaintive in his goldfish footie jammies.

"Shut up, shithead," Brett said. "You're lucky I don't toss your ass out with her."

"Don't talk to that boy thataway," Ruby said. She could feel the baton in her pocket hard against her thigh.

"Don't say nothing, jailbird," Brett said, tone amiable. "You ain't got a goddamn word to say about anything I say. Not in my house. Not now or ever." He swiveled on his stool. "Where were you planning on housing the jailbird, honey?"

"I was going to give her Leo's room," Ivy said.

"They can share. I don't need shithead there crawling up in my bed again, kicking me in the nuts."

"Fine by me," Ruby said.

"Good. Now why don't you get on back to the back before I start slapping some sense into people around here. Both of yous."

Ruby started to say something but stopped when she saw Ivy's pleading face. So instead she held Leo's hand back to Leo's room. In a singlewide trailer this was not a long walk but it still took all her effort not to squeeze Leo's hand so hard she hurt the boy.

Leo's room was close and dark, the more comforting for the fact. Seven years and six months she'd passed in close, dark places. A few more hours wouldn't hurt. Creaky walls sadly hung with a poster of Ichiro Suzuki and a lion, the kind of creased posters that come out of cereal boxes. These covered most but not all of the holes. For Leo's bed, a mattress on the floor and for his chest of drawers, a stack of laundry baskets. There were burns in the carpets and aluminum foil hung over on the window. Ruby remembered that trick well enough, the way to keep out the light when you didn't want to face the day. She knew everything about this room. She'd done all her growing up in places just like it.

Little Leo sat cross-legged on the mattress on the floor and smiled up at her. Ruby set her sling bag down and sat beside him, mattress sagging badly with her weight. She put an arm around the boy who snuggled his tiny frame and mammal heat into her.

"Aunt Ruby," he said, "do you know any songs?"

"Sure I do," Ruby said.

"Will you sing them to me?"

From the front of the trailer Ruby could hear Brett and Ivy arguing. Leo seemed unfazed. Ruby supposed it wasn't anything like his first time.

"You bet. That what your mama does at nights? Sing you songs?"

"Sometimes."

"Well, now. I'll sing to you. Your Aunt Ruby will sing to you."

Ruby sang the songs she knew, surprised that "Mama Tried" and "Rainy Day Woman" and "Pancho and Lefty" leapt up from her memory. She could smell Daddy's whiskey breath with the rhymes, feel his scratchy whiskers on her cheek.

When Leo fell asleep, she laid down next to him on the narrow mattress. A lamp sat on the thin carpet beside the mattress and she flicked it on on and off, on and off. In Chowchilla there were no light switches. It went dark when they said so, light when they said so. Ruby kept on playing with the lamp till the bulb burned out with a soft sizzle.

◇◇◇◇◇◇

Some time later crashing and screams jarred Ruby from sleep. At first she didn't know she was in Leo's room. She didn't know she was in the trailer. She didn't know she was in Barstow. She thought she was back in Chowchilla, some guard down the corridor welcoming a new fish to life in prison with some beating and raping. She didn't move, she didn't sit up. Number one rule in Chowchilla, never attract attention to yourself. Even when one of those guards came to visit your cell, you never moved. You never said a damn word.

Then she felt Leo's warm breath on her cheek, his animal warmth against her ribs, Ichiro Suzuki with his bat looking down on them like a wise old god. It all came back to her. Down the hall echoed shattering glass and Ivy screaming. Leo went on slumbering. None of this bothered him a bit. She thought about that a minute, how a boy of his age could sleep through such a ruckus.

Then she cast aside the lingering prison paralysis, snicked out the Prather to full length and barreled down the hall. Sap in hand just like the old days.

The overhead light above the kitchen counter swung on a crazy arc, casting jumping shadows. Brett loomed over Ivy crumpled and covering her face like she knew what was coming. Brett's fists were clenched and he looked like he sure did, too.

He never got the chance. No, not this time. Ruby swung that sap faster than the bouncing shadows. A crack against Brett's temple and the man keeled over like a stack of wet lumber, head crunching against the countertop corner and flopping onto a spaghetti sauce stain on the linoleum. The guitar case toppled off the other side of the counter.

Ivy looked out from behind her elbows and up at her little sister, holding out a hand. While she let Ruby help her to her feet Brett quit flopping around, blood pooling over the spaghetti stain, eyes flipped open and rolled back to their whites. The two sisters stood over him till he finally went still.

"Did you ...?" Ivy said. "Is he ...?"

Ruby knelt by the man though she already knew. Felt for a pulse anyway.

"He's gone," she said.

"Ah Christ, Ruby!" Ivy said. "What have you done?"

"You a big goddamn favor, is what," Ruby said.

Ivy laced her fingers at the back of her head and walked to the front window hung with a Minnesota Vikings blanket for a curtain. Ruby followed her. Noticed she was still gripping the Prather when she reached for her sister so she tried to slip it into her pocket and this was when she noticed that Brett's guitar case had popped open. There was no guitar inside.

"I knew this was going to happen some day, I just knew it," Ivy said, still circling the room, ignoring her sister. "This or something goddamn like it."

"Ivy."

"I just didn't think it would be . . . Oh Christ."

"Ivy."

"Now what are we going to do?"

"Ivy!"

Ivy turned and the "What?!!?" died on her lips. Instead she said, "Is that?"

"Don't touch it," Ruby said.

A dozen identical white bundles wrapped in light blue plastic spilled out of the guitar case onto the floor.

"Oh my God," Ivy said.

"You said he was small time," Ruby said.

"He was!" Ivy said.

"This ain't small-time. This is the kind of shit people come looking for."

The two sisters stood over the scene, the dead man, the narcotics, the trailer.

"Russians, you said?" Ruby said.

Ivy nodded.

"We got to leave it. Leave it alone and get out of here. Hope to hell they won't care about us."

"Sure, sure. Moon Pie, what do you ... what do you think this is all worth?"

"Don't go getting any stupid ideas, Banana Bean. Because it's worth enough for them to come after it. And whatever that number is, it ain't worth your life. Leo's life."

"No," Ivy said. "No, of course not."

"We got to think this through. We got to do this right. And if you touch that stuff even once, they'll never stop coming after us."

As if on cue the phone in Brett's pocket went off. The dial tone was "Bulls on Parade," Rage Against The Machine.

"See what I mean?" Ruby said. "We ain't got much time."

"You think they'll let us go?"

"Not if we're here when they get here. So we best not be."

"All right," Ivy said softly. Looked over Brett again. "Funny, you know. I was just sort of getting to like it here." She walked around the counter to the kitchen and kicked Brett's unlaced black boot. "Dickhead," she said. "I can't believe you did it again, Moon Pie. Instead of me. Again."

Ruby put an arm around her sister's shoulders. "How about you make it so there's no more 'again' for either of us. Ever." She turned for the back room, cataloguing everywhere she'd been in the trailer. "You got any money?"

Ivy shook her head. "Fifty bucks, maybe. A hundred. You?"

"Three hundred and seventy-seven bucks and eighty cents. Which ain't going to get us very far down the road."

"I know where we can get some money."

"Where?"

"You ain't going to like it."

"Where, Ivy?"

Ivy heaved a deep sigh. "The 'End."

"What?"

"Back in the 'End, Moon Pie."

"Fucking Wyoming? Are you shitting me?"

"Shhh, shhh," Ivy said, jutting a chin at the back-room. The sisters listened, but no sound came from Leo's room. "I'm serious, Moon Pie. I got five grand stashed back there."

"You're going to have to explain that to me."

"I went with Brett on one of his runs. Out to Chicago and back."

"You went with that sack of shit one of his drug runs?"

Ivy shrugged. "We were smoking a lot of crank."

"We."

"I quit now, Moon Pie. Anyway, that's how I know he works for the Russians."

"Worked. And all that means is that they know who you are, too."

"Yeah. God, that's right."

"Go on. You were saying something about five grand."

"Well, on that trip, I told Brett I wanted to stop back home. Haven't been there in years, I said. He always did get a kick out of me being from Wyoming. What the hell, he said, and drove us there." She looked at his twisted ankles there on the cheap linoleum. "I could talk him into most anything once he started toking up. He wasn't all that bad a guy sometimes, you know."

"Whatever. So you actually went back to the house?"

"Yes we did. Drove right up Burma Road. It's abandoned now, Moon Pie. No one lives there. The way the place was falling apart, probably no one's been living there for years. Brett went out back to piss and roll us up a joint, you know out back by the shed?"

"Uh-huh. This is a great story, Banana Bean, but would you come to the point?"

"I'm getting there! I always thought a day like this would come, you know. But what the hell was I supposed to do, try to hide money in this shithole?

So I took a cashbox from the car, and hid it in the house."

"Seriously?"

"It seemed like a good idea at the time. And it seems like one hell of a good one right now. I walked right in the house and upstairs and back in that crawl space off our old bedroom. The third rafter. You remember, the one I carved a heart in?"

"I remember."

"I hid it back there. Insurance policy, I figured. Figured someday I might need it." She put her arms on Ruby's shoulders. "Today's that day, Moon Pie."

"Sure looks like it," Ruby said. "And Brett never noticed."

"Oh, he noticed. I convinced him later that some-one had stole it out of the car at some gas station back in Iowa. Christ, he was pissed."

"How much, again?"

"Five grand. Maybe more. Maybe seven." She rubbed her nose. "Funny thing, you know. That cash box? Kind of reminded me of the one in Mrs. Custer's office."

"Ha. No shit."

"Fuck em, right, little sister?"

"That's right," Ruby said. "Fuck em."

◇◇◇◇◇◇

www.ingramcontent.com/pod-product-compliance
Lightning Source LLC
Chambersburg PA
CBHW051828170626
46807CB00003B/1078